# Between You & Me

## & Me

### Real-life Diaries and Letters by Women Writers
### Charlotte Cole, editor

LiveWiRE

A big thank you to all the writers who sent me their letters and diaries; and thanks also to everyone at The Women's Press who helped me with this book.

published by Livewire Books, The Women's Press Ltd, 1998
member of the Namara Group
Great Sutton Street, London EC1V 0DX

collection copyright © The Women's Press 1998

The copyright in each of the pieces in this collection remains with the original copyright holder.

The extract on pp63–67 is reprinted from *The Letters of Charlotte Brontë: Volume One 1829–1847* edited by Margaret Smith (1995) by permission of Oxford University Press.

The extract on pp89–95 is reprinted from *Diary of a Young Girl: Definitive Edition* by Anne Frank (1997) by permission of Penguin UK and the Anne Frank-Fonds.

The extract on pp68–76 is reprinted from *Katherine Mansfield: Selected Letters* edited by Vincent O'Sullivan (1989) by permission of Oxford University Press.

The extract on pp21–24 is reprinted from *Letters Home: Correspondence 1950–1963* by Sylvia Plath (1976) by permission of Faber & Faber Ltd and HarperCollins Publishers USA.

The extract on pp45–50 is reprinted from *The Letters of Mary Wollstonecraft Shelley: Volume I* edited by Betty T Bennett (1988) by permission of The John Watkins University Press.

The extract on pp50–56 is reprinted from *A Passionate Apprentice: The Early Journals* by Virginia Woolf (1990) by permission of Random House UK and Harcourt Brace and Company USA.

The right of the contributors to be identified as the joint authors of this work has been asserted by them in accordance with the Copyright, Designs and Patents Act 1988.

British Library Cataloguing-in-Publication Data
A catalogue record for this book is available from the British Library.

ISBN 0 7043 4955 8

Typeset in 12/14pt Bembo by FSH Ltd, London
Printed and bound in Great Britain by Cox & Wyman Ltd,
Reading, Berkshire

# Contents

## Family

## Relationships

# Foreword

Most people have kept a diary at some stage in their lives. We want to record what is going on in our world; to express our most intimate thoughts and feelings. We want to find out who we are, and what we want to be. And at times, when the worst or unimaginable happens, we can find it tremendously comforting to write everything down.

Of course, we usually share some of these things with our closest friends and family. When there is a separation, even the most steadfast of relationships can drift apart, and journals can be a great help in this difficult period. If a correspondence is begun, however, the relationship often grows *stronger* — as there can actually be more space to talk honestly about our hopes and fears on paper, than face to face in the midst of daily life.

Women, always the best communicators, are prolific diary and letter writers – and they often begin as young women, when life is at its most exciting. Perhaps not surprisingly, some of the most captivating and poignant of these early writings are by women who have then gone on to become professional writers, and it was with this in mind that I put together *Between You and Me*. It is always interesting to look back over your own treasured letters and old diaries – but to read other people's is much more intriguing! Editing this collection, I have found it to be extremely touching and inspiring too.

From Christine Purkis battling with exams to Kate Cann looking for the perfect boyfriend; from Charlotte Brontë reflecting on her life as a governess to Mary Wollstonecraft Shelley narrating her beautiful and wild trip through the Alps; each letter and diary extract in *Between You and Me* reveals a privileged and fascinating insight into the lives of these women writers.

Charlotte Cole

# School

*Love it or hate it, school is a part of all our lives and we have to get through it somehow!*

*Exams are the worst time for everyone, and Christine Purkis was no exception! She attended a high-achieving academic school, where if you were anything less than an A grade student you certainly felt the strain. There was little opportunity for anything other than revision – except for dreaming, of course . . .*

## Christine Purkis, aged 15

Thursday 8 February, 1962
Woken at six o'clock – unfortunately – because I was having a super dream about Jess Harper from the cowboy serial *Laramie*, and I've decided I have a great big crush on him. Don't know anyone in real life half as handsome as Jess. Don't know anyone at all come to think of it. Art exam – I found it was composition, not life. I did two men fishing including boat, picnic basket, bottle and bowler hat. It was lousy. Oh dear – I'd hoped that art would be one of my better ones. Got home about six and worked till supper then watched programme about Afghanistan. After news went to bed about 9.30.

Friday 9 February
Had German 'diktat' first lesson. It could have been much worse but even so I got lots of mistakes. Biology lesson on bones. I stepped on a very rare kind and broke it! Netball last lesson. I didn't muck around but Miss Purdie made us all stay in for ten minutes after the bell.

Tuesday 13 February
Off to school with chocolate for mock exams. Started

with English essay. Very strange in the hall but got used to it. Wrote on *Road to the Coast* but was very rushed so I expect it's full of careless mistakes. Straight into Arithmetic – awful. Couldn't do any of it. One definite fail. Home – whacked. Struggled to revise History. Bed after the news but decided I didn't know anything so did more revision in bed.

Monday 19 February
Biology exam. Awful paper – very difficult and twisted questions. After lunch – plant drawing – daffodil and a twig – very enjoyable. Revised Scripture all evening. Watched half of *Panorama* – floods in Hamburg, 150 feared dead. New stage in Algerian cease-fire but I don't understand it.

Tuesday 20 February
Geometry exam not as bad as I expected. Nice lunch. Awful Scripture exam. None of the stuff I'd learnt. Great excitement as Colonel Glen's rocket was in orbit. Looked at special report about his splash down in the Atlantic.

Wednesday 28 February
Great general excitement over results. Got B for German. I was disappointed but I knew I'd done the paper badly. B for Scripture. Again disappointing – everyone else got B+. Arithmetic D – very disappointing, Miss Tame said I must have lost my head. At last it was Jess's night on *Laramie*. Swoon!!

Memorandum
Well, it went. I never thought I'd get through and it's over

now. Not as bad as I expected. In fact I enjoyed the exams. It's the revision – I'm just allergic to work. And the marks. Wish I wasn't such a B person. Between work; some good times. Friends good from all points of view. Crush on Jess fully launched. Get scared at nights – I'm just a baby. I must learn the dark's nothing to be afraid of – and the noise of the window too.

Resolutions:

*Diet:* resolved to keep to it from Saturday 3 March. No eating in between meals except two biscuits at 11 am. No sweets. Small breakfast with Vita Wheat. Small helpings at midday. Little potato. One lot of second helpings per week. Healthy evening meal but low starch. Cut down generally but not drastically.

*For Lent*

Give up:  Biscuits 1) At school to save money for refugees
2) As a group at church to save money
3) In any other way for personal discipline.
Biting nails – for self-discipline
Sweets for discipline and diet reasons.

Thursday 14 March

French conversation class with Miss Ellis before school. Usual lessons. Had audition for Ismeme in *Antigone*. Not too good. After supper, worked, listened to Lux. Watched *Laramie* in pyjamas. Jess's night. But very slushy. Couldn't watch. How frustrating it is to adore a person I'm never likely to even see in my real life.

Saturday 16 June
Yet another ghastly night − over five hours getting to sleep. Went with Mum to the doctor's and he prescribed me sleeping pills. Worked all morning. After lunch worked again − dead beat and found it difficult to concentrate. Watched *Juke Box Jury* and then went out with friends. Home. Took pill. Here's to a night's sleep.

Wednesday 21 June
Study leave. Worked all day and after supper till eight. Felt I'd done a lot of work. I so hope I remember it. Watched programme on Wimbledon seeds. Bed at 9.30. Well, here goes. GCEs, the things I thought would never happen, are really here. God, help me please.

Thursday 21 June
Several Good Luck cards. Worked at home all morning. School dinner. Lindy very irritating about being proud she hadn't done any work. Exam not bad. Wrote all about Scotland but didn't have time to read it through. Very dangerous. Read History in bed. God, please let it return to me tomorrow. I honestly don't know what I know.

Friday 22 June
Ghastly History. Much worse than I expected. Still, it's over. Wrote reams. English language précis difficult . . . all I can think is that they're over. Absolutely whacked.

Monday 25 June
Geometry exam. Danny Greene sick just behind my desk in the hall. I felt queasy and wobbly at the knees. Exam ghastly. Well, it was a fair paper, but I did hopelessly. Was

in despair. Daddy encouraging and reckons I've just scraped through. Wish I felt the same. Television went wrong. Light out at 9.15.

Friday 31 August
Woken by Mummy at eight. I knew what she'd come for. Wouldn't open it though. She went but Daddy came up and said if I wouldn't open it, he would — so I did and I nearly died! I got all of them.

*In 1940, there was not only the School Certificate to revise for, but also World War II to contend with! Joan Aiken was at a boarding school in Oxford, and in these letters to her sister in the USA, the war seems to be more of a diversion from the routine of studying than anything else! Miss Snodgrass, I have been assured, is alive and well and still living in Oxford — and receives copies of all Joan's books.*

**Joan Aiken, aged 16**

Wychwood
Summer 1940

Dear Jane,
  . . . Miss Snodgrass has worked out that if I want to take College Entrance for Somerville I can work for it this next year and take it in November which seems pretty neat. The only thing is, I still don't really know what I want to do. I like English by far the best but I don't want to spoil it by doing it. But I am not sure that I like chemistry well enough to do really. What do you think? Anyway it doesn't matter yet . . .

. . . Four of us went for a picnic the other day. We lay in the fields beside the river and slept and ate. I have come to the conclusion that that is the only thing that one ought to do at Oxford in the summer. It is half term next weekend, and the Government won't let schools let children go home, so we shall all be staying. We have a full weekend before us! We are going to see *Murder in the Cathedral* done by Christ Church in its cloisters, and a Shaw play; and we are going to bathe a lot; and go down the river in punts as far as Willingford and have lunch there, and we want to have a moonlight bathe, but unfortunately there is no moon.

Your descriptions of American food made me quite tearful! Actually the school food has benefited by the war in one way, because now, instead of the rather green and greasy jam which we used to have, we have Maple Syrup, which of course beats it to a cocked hat.

The awful thing at the moment is that Miss Snodgrass is leaving, which really is tragic, because she has done, and is doing, a terrible lot for Wychwood, and knows more about it than anyone. Besides she is extremely nice. Ruth is completely heartbroken, and determines to leave at Christmas, but I think that would be rather excessive, I must say!

What a good thing you aren't at home, or you would be departed of all cameras, bicycles, watches, spectacles and whatnot, and made to go to bed at nine every night. A depressing prospect indeed . . . Today, as it was the last Form Meeting day before half term, my form discussed me in my capacity of form representative, and said many rude things about me, but decided to keep me on. The trouble is I hate ordering people around!

Since your letter another one came – this morning to be precise. It seemed to be written a week earlier. Very curious? Thank you very much for it too! I really ought to stop, having said nothing at all, and anyway I also suspect that long letters from me are more of a pain than a pleasure!

With love from Joan

Autumn 1940

Dear Jane,

. . . Drawing is rather dull at the moment because we are learning to do still life, but every now and then I break out into a savage poster. It is horrible being confined to a syllabus. 'Specially in English where we spend our time doing odious exercises instead of nice essays.

I am in the first hockey team. How surprising! But I enjoy myself thoroughly and even occasionally shoot a goal.

I am very hungry because I have not had any tea, being too busy doing I don't remember what. We have fish pie for supper on Fridays and stewed apples. We have taken to having dripping at tea, which I love because the school butter always had a sinister flavour of margarine anyway.

I won a prize for poetry at the Oxford Institute of Psychology. It was a book token, so I got David *The Midnight Folk* by Masefield. Did you ever read it? I read him the *The Box of Delights* last holidays, having taken it back from school and he liked it so much I thought *The Midnight Folk* would be a safe present. He is just as fussy about the books he has read to him as ever.

Miss Snodgrass has three Siamese kittens which she is looking after. They are very wild and climb around on the furniture in the most dangerous way, so that they look rather like the Thurber drawing: 'We have cats the way some people have mice'. The largest of them is in here at the moment sitting on the mantelpiece and staring with great, plum-coloured eyes at the Virginia Creeper stems which are rattling outside the window.

I am taking Ann Mullins to church this morning, that being one of the privileges of a citizen. Silly that we used to *miss* church together and now we walk solemnly and respectfully down with our prayer books and sing very loud.

By the way you haven't said whether there is a cat in your Divinities. I hope you have a lovely birthday!

With love from Joan

6 December 1940

Dear Jane,

Merry Christmas! I hope this letter arrives at pretty nearly the right date, and finds you doing all the appropriate things, eating turkey and being lost in the snow — does it snow with you at the moment? We had one snowstorm the other day, but it didn't lie of course; however our Geography mistress says that we are entering into another cold age, which is comforting. It is an awful pity that you weren't at Sutton last year to see the superb snow there, because even if *you* had it *much* deeper, snow is always nicer at home don't you think? Anyhow, to return to the point, I hope you have a perfectly lovely Christmas with your family there in spirit, if not in body, that is if you like that sort of thing of course! Far be it for me to doom you to an awful day of wandering round, haunted by family: 'Who's that distressed looking person?' 'Oh that's Jane Aiken; I wouldn't go near her if I were you, because you will only be pinched by the ghosts of her family. They are so selfish, the poor girl can't get away from them.'

I am sorry about the shortage of letters, but I really have had very little time; the school are so terribly anxious not to let our form fail in School Certificate – you heard about the last awful failures, didn't you? — that they are having fairly hard on us. One girl has already done her best by having a nervous breakdown. I don't do that, because I recite poetry in bed at night instead of dates and formulae, and spend my Saturday evenings drawing instead of composing chronologies, but it is a near thing. The atmosphere is slightly worse at the moment because of exams – mostly trial School Cert. papers of course, so that I simply can't prevent myself from dreaming about kings and relative density, but I play games very hard to counteract that. The only disadvantage is that I was found reading History in bed last week, with the result that I have to get up at seven and do things by way of punishment, and I am liable to oversleep if I play games too hard. The punishments themselves are very good for me however! One was writing out the *Ancient Mariner* in beautiful writing, and there have been things like learning all the Latin numbers and things like principle parts, and the kings of England and their dates and wives.

Besides all these useful diversions we sing carols and act Christmas plays and play hockey energetically. I like hockey much better than lacrosse, but that is probably because we never got beyond tests with lacrosse.

There is not going to be a Magazine this term, as Miss Lee thinks it is hard on the printers and a waste of paper and whatnot. But things are going to be written very beautifully on decorated brown paper, or something to that effect, by the Juniors, and passed round the school, and shown to admiring parents. I doubt if I shall have anything in, because the essay I wrote was on the Spanish war – very bloodthirsty and most unsuitable! However, I enjoyed writing it, which is the main thing isn't it? (My writing is going to pieces, as you will notice. I had better learn to type.)

I think I ought to stop and revise my science!

> With love and another Merry Christmas from
> Joan

*Being the 'new girl' is a difficult time for anyone, and coming from the 'posh' school in Bath didn't help Tamara Sturtz much either! Tamara knew that skipping school for two years wasn't the best option, so she eventually worked out an alternative – and one that would keep her parents happy too . . .*

### Tamara Sturtz, aged 17

Sunday 5 January, 1986
Went over to Alex's house and listened to records. We braved a walk but it was too cold. Had a lovely, relaxing day. Came home and did some taping for Kate.

Monday 6 January
School. Went to Binks Café at lunchtime. Waited for Alex

but he didn't turn up. He wasn't at work either. Rang him when I got home and he was ill.

Found that the tech can't have me, their art courses are too full. I've come up with another idea. Drop 'A' levels and do an art foundation course next year and work somewhere in the meantime. Mum seemed quite keen.

Tuesday 7 January

Didn't go to school today. Went to the tech for a prospectus but they don't do a foundation course. Met Alex at lunchtime. Went to Sydney Place art college and got an application form for their foundation course. I've got to do an entrance test. Met Rachel and Jill in Binks. Rang Jessica in the evening but she was rather unsociable as usual.

Wednesday 8 January

School. Met Alex at lunchtime. Went to the careers office with mum. They said I should do 'A' levels. I came out in a foul mood. Mum spoke to Dad this evening. It seems that he has made my decision for me: to take my 'A' levels even if I get into Sydney Place. Mum says she hasn't taken sides but it's obvious she has. Trust him to interfere. God, I hate him sometimes. Mum's not even talking to me now.

Saturday 11 January

Went into Bath with Kate and took some photographs for my art project. Mum's new boyfriend, John, came over in the evening. Did some English homework and watched TV.

I now understand why I should do 'A' levels – without

them I won't be able to go to college or get a really good job – but I only wish to God I didn't have to do them at Hayesfield. It's like a prison. Whatever I do, however hard I try, I can't seem to get out. There's always something or someone to stop me!

Monday 13 January
School. Went into Bath at break. I was walking up Milsom Street and I saw Rich walking towards me – he's so brown. He came back from Bali yesterday. He looked gorgeous. He asked if I'd like to go for a cup of tea so we went to Binks. He had a lot to talk about. Alex came in and Rich left. I was in such a good mood. Alex came to the bank with me and then I went back up to school.

Wednesday 15 January
Art exam. I've done one hour, I think it's going to be okay. Went to Binks at lunchtime. Rich came in but he was sitting with a friend. He looked round and grinned a couple of times though. Alex came in. Went back up to school and asked if I could go home. Met Harriet in Binks. I have decided at last between Alex and Rich: Rich, if I can get him! I'm sick of Alex messing me around – either he wants to go out with me or he doesn't – and Rich is so gorgeous.

Friday 24 January
School. Met Harriet at lunchtime. She saw Rich last night and he told her that he really likes me but he met a girl in Bali and he just can't go out with anyone at the moment. I thought that was quite a strange thing for him to say because I'm supposed to be going out with Alex anyway.

Wednesday 12 February
Met Harriet and Alex in Binks. When Alex left, Rachel came in. There was great conflict between her and Harriet. I don't know what's going on. Went shopping with Rachel. Bought a Valentine's card for Alex.

Friday 14 February
Went into town with Kate as she was having her hair bleached. Sat in the hairdresser's for two hours.

Kate came round this evening and we went up to the Assembly pub. Alex, James, Nick and Rachel were there. I got very drunk. Alex was talking to that girl Sarah from Hayesfield. Just as we were leaving I asked if it was over between us and he said it would be better if we were really good friends in the long run – so really nothing's changed. I don't mind who he goes out with as long as it's not Sarah. It's funny how Alex and I split up on Valentine's day.

Monday 24 February
School. Met Jill, Rachel and Harriet at lunchtime. Sweeney Todds are advertising in the paper for waitresses so I rang them. I'm going in to see them after school tomorrow.

Tuesday 25 February
Went to Sweeney Todds after school and I'm working for three hours on Thursday and then again on Saturday.

Mum and I went to John's for supper. Met Paul who's fifteen, and Clare who's nineteen. She cooked the supper. It was really uneasy and very polite at first but everyone began to relax a bit later on.

## Thursday 27 February
School. Met everyone in Binks at lunchtime. As soon as Rachel came in, Harriet walked out. It was really funny. Rachel can't stand Harriet. I have to agree she is really annoying sometimes.

I was working in Sweeney Todds this evening until 9 pm. It was really good fun. Afterwards I sat down and had a pizza and a coffee. Everyone was really nice.

## Friday 28 February
School. Met everyone in Binks at lunchtime. Jessica was in there. James Courtney came in and sat with Jessica. I tried to avoid him but Jessica called me over. Apparently he'd asked Jessica if I was going to be in Bath tomorrow. It's a pity he's so weird; he's very good-looking.

Kate came round this evening and we went out. Went to the Underground with Kate and Rachel. There was an absolutely gorgeous blond guy there. He was tall and gorgeous and kept staring. When Kate was getting her coat he wouldn't stop staring and grinning at me, right until we were out of the nightclub.

## Saturday 1 March
Stayed in all day and went to work at 5.30 pm. Robert was on the same shift. He's quite a bit older and has a girlfriend, but he's so nice. He asked if I was going to Moles after work, but I was going to the Underground with Kate. Later on he said that it was a pity I wasn't going to Moles, then he said 'maybe some other time'. I couldn't believe it. We didn't finish until 1.30 am. Kate came to meet me but I was too tired to go out so I went home.

Easter Monday 31 March
Went to work. It was very busy because of the bank holiday. After work I went to Evelyn's with Robert and he bought me a drink. Saw Jill and Rachel. Robert and I got on really well and I had a brilliant evening. Mum suddenly appeared in an absolutely foul mood because she didn't know where I was. I was so embarrassed. She'd rung Kate who'd rung Alex, God knows why. She stormed out. Robert said I should rebel and go to Moles with him; he offered to pay. I had to tell him not to tempt me. Got a taxi home. John was there, thank goodness. I really apologised and everything's okay now.

Tuesday 1 April
Just before I went to work, had a huge argument with Mum. I was almost late for work. Went to Moles with Robert afterwards. He said he'd really enjoyed seeing me last night. Got a taxi home and found a note from Mum saying that I have to cancel working on Thursday night. I can't believe it.

Wednesday 2 April
Went to work. We were so busy and I was in tears all day because of Mum. They were really sweet though. Got home and had another massive row with Mum. She says I'm selfish and that I'm working in the restaurant too much, not working properly at school, and that I never help her around the house. She threw a lemon at me. I went up to clean my room and knocked a glass bottle over. I was so angry and upset that I threw it at the wall and it made a huge hole. Well, that will serve her right. Anyway, everything's sorted out now and I'm working

tomorrow but from now on I'm only allowed to do one shift a weekend. I hope they agree.

Tuesday 8 April
It all blew up today. Went to school and left after the first lesson. Met Jill in Binks. Just as I was leaving I bumped into Mum. Typical. She went absolutely mad and said that she was going to have a nervous breakdown because of me.

We talked about it this evening and I told her how much I hate Hayesfield and how miserable it's making me. She's agreed that I can go to the tech part-time next year and do my 'A' levels in a year there, which also means I can carry on working at Sweeney Todds. I can't believe it, I'm so happy.

Tuesday 15 April
Left school after English and went into town. As I was at the cashpoint I saw Mrs Wakefield (head of sixth form) walking down the street. I ran round the corner and hoped she hadn't seen me. I thought I'd better go back up to school after lunch. Mrs Wakefield called me into her office and said she'd seen me in town. I told her that I'd been to the tech to get information about courses for next year because I was leaving. She told me she knew I wasn't happy at Hayesfield and thought it was best that I left. I suppose I'm kind of being expelled, except that I was going anyway. Dad certainly can't interfere now.

Friday 16 May
School. My last day! Went home after lunch and sat in the garden *all* afternoon.

# Ambitions

*Some people seem to know what they want to be right from an early age, whereas others decide later on. Others still are happy just to see what life brings to them . . .*

*Sylvia Plath always wanted to be a writer. In the following letters to her mother she balances college work and socialising with developing her writing career. For Sylvia an important part of the writing process was to be published and receive money to help with her college expenses, so she astutely wrote stories for women's magazines and poetry for literary magazines. Despite some rejections she often had great success . . .*

**Sylvia Plath, aged 19**

7 February, 1952

As you may imagine, I felt pretty low today when I got my [*rejection*] letter from *Seventeen*. I hadn't realised the subconscious support I was getting from thinking of what I would do with my $500. I guess I'll really have to hit those True Stories. By the way, I suddenly got an inspiration for the 'Civic Activities' section of my application blank. I am starting next Monday to teach art to a class of kids at the People's Institute, volunteer work (make it sound impressive). Next year I hope for either mental or veterans hospital . . . I feel suddenly very untalented as I look at my slump of work in art and writing. Am I destined to deteriorate for the rest of my life? . . . *Do* write for Dr Christian. [*The radio show had a writing contest.*] Every year you will, until you win. You have the background and technical terms. Go to it!

7 March, 1952

Maybe your daughter is slightly crazy, maybe she just takes after her illustrious mother, but in spite of the fact she has three wicked writtens next week, she is just now feeling . . . very virtuous because she refused three weekends this weekend – Frosh Prom at Yale, Junior Prom at Princeton, and a blind date from MIT . . .

Just finished delivering my best baby yet – a story (only 7 pp) about a vet with one leg missing and a girl meeting on a train. Dialogue discipline, you know . . .

10 April, 1952

Got straight A on that old English exam I took way back when, with a 'This is an excellent paper' from the august Elizabeth Drew herself! So happy I didn't go to Princeton. Last night I sat up to type the 16-page story 'Sunday at the Mintons" that I'm sending to *Mlle* just for fun. You would be interested to see the changes. I made it a psychological type thing, wish-fulfilment, etc. so it wouldn't be at all far-fetched. Tonight I hear Robert Frost, tomorrow, Senator McCarthy. Also wrote two poems this weekend which I'll send eventually: 'Go Get the Goodly Squab in Goldlobed Corn' . . . Life is terribly rushed what with Press Board, work, and all these lectures – but fun.

30 April, 1952

You are listening to the most busy and happy girl in the world. Today is one of those when every little line falls in pleasant places.

. . . I have just been elected to Alpha Phi Kappa Psi, which is the Phi Beta Kappa of the Arts. So I am one of the two sophs chosen for creative writing ability! We all got single roses and marched out in chapel today. Also, I think I will get at least one sonnet published in the erudite *Smith Review* this next fall!

. . . at the first Alpha meeting after lunch today two girls came running up to me and said how would I like to be on the Editorial Board of the *Smith Review* next year, and my, how they just loved my sonnet: Eva. (What a life!)

. . . None other than WH Auden, the famous modern poet, is to come to Smith next year (along with Vera Michelis Dean) and may teach English, or possibly creative writing! So I hope to petition to get into one of his classes. (Imagine saying, 'Oh, yes, I studied writing under Auden!')

. . . Honestly, Mum, I could just cry with happiness. I love this place so, and there is so much to do creatively, without having to be a 'club woman'. Fie upon offices! The world is splitting open at my feet like a ripe, juicy watermelon. If only I can work, work, work to justify all my opportunities.

Your happy girl,
Sivvy

The Bellmont Hotel, Cape Cod
11 June, 1952

Your amazing telegram came just as I was scrubbing tables in the shady interior of The Belmont dining room.

I was so excited that I screamed and actually threw my arms around the head waitress who no doubt thinks I am rather insane! Anyhow, psychologically, the moment couldn't have been better. I felt tired first night's sleep in new places never *are* peaceful and I didn't get much! To top it off, I was the only girl waitress here, and had been scrubbing furniture, washing dishes and silver, lifting tables, etc since 8am. Also I just learned since I am completely inexperienced, I am not going to be working in the main dining room, but in the 'side hall' where the managers and top hotel brass eat. So, tips will no doubt net much less during the summer and the company be less interesting. So I was beginning to worry about money when your telegram came. God! To think 'Sunday at the Mintons'' is *one* of *two* prize stories to be put in a big national slick!!! Frankly, I can't believe it!

The first thing I thought of was: Mother can keep her intersession money and buy some pretty clothes and a special trip or something! At least I get a winter coat and extra special suit out of the Mintons. I *think* the prize is $500!!!!!!!!!

ME! Of all people . . .

So it's really looking up around here, now that I don't have to be scared stiff about money . . . Oh, I say, even if my feet kill me after this first week, and I drop 20 trays, I will have the beach, boys to bring me beer, sun, and young gay companions. What a life.

Love, your crazy old daughter. (Or as Eddie said: 'One hell of a sexy dame'!)

xxx Sivvy

*Juliet Gellatley 'fell' into being a writer through her work for animals. These extracts from her diaries show how she gradually became aware of the abuses animals suffer, and how — despite the disinterest and mockery of friends parents and teachers — she was determined to try and end it.*

## Juliet Gellatley, aged 13–16

May, 1977
Monday
A gorgeous tabby cat keeps meowing outside my bedroom window. She climbs on to the extension roof and jumps on to my window sill. The only trouble is my mum doesn't want another cat and Pusina, my beautiful black half Siamese, hates her.

Thursday
It's funny really. I have to sneak food upstairs without anyone seeing. Tonight my mum came into my room but thank God, Almaz (that's what I've called the tabby) was under my bed. I tried to act normal, but had to talk non-stop and quite loud so she wouldn't hear her eating!!!

Saturday
Mum asked me why the cat food was running out so fast. I tried to look bored and didn't answer.

Friday
Omigod! She's had kittens. Almaz has had THREE KITTENS in my wardrobe. I'll have to tell Mum.

Saturday

Aaaaaah the kittens are soooooo cute. There's one black and two tabbies. Their eyes are tightly shut and they are so helpless. I told Mum and Dad last night. I was so scared they might say they've got to go that first I asked them what they thought of people who just got rid of kittens 'cos they were a nuisance. I really laid it on how cruel it was and they agreed. I said to Mum: 'You'd never do anything like that, would you?' and she said: 'What do you think I am?' So then I told them. They actually laughed and were great about it – I should have known really.

June

Saturday

I feel really sad and have been crying. Eenie, Meenie and Mo, my three beautiful kittens, have all gone. I know they're going to good homes but all the same, I'll really miss them. They were so much fun. See, I'm already writing about them like they've gone for ever. At least I'll still be able to see Mo, who has only gone across the road to a neighbour. Eenie and Meenie have gone to two of Mum's friends who I know love animals so I suppose I'll get regular progress reports. Almaz doesn't seem to mind, though. I think she'd had enough of them. I've found out where she came from – it's a really rough-looking house two streets away. Anyway, she's here now and Mum has paid for her to be spayed. Best thing, I suppose, but kittens are just so cute.

Thursday

I can't believe it! Almaz has gone back to her old home. She only came to us to have her kittens! Of all the ungrateful . . . Mum said: 'You don't choose cats, they choose you!' I guess she's right but I am going to miss her. Maybe she'll come back again.

April, 1978
Saturday
I picked up some leaflets from a stall in the precinct today and it is DISGUSTING. I hate the human race!!! It's all about snaring foxes and how they strangle themselves or die of starvation. I can't believe it but farmers are allowed to do it. I've got to join the RSPCA now! I've got to try and stop it. I'll ask Mum if she'll lend me the money because I'm broke. I was out with Stephen and very late home last night so today is NOT a good day to ask her. I'll do it tomorrow.

May
Tuesday
Received my membership from the RSPCA and a copy of their youth mag called *Animal World*. It's really great. So there are other people who feel like I do! I'm not a weirdo after all. There's a petition to fill in against snaring and they want me to get as many people to sign it as I can. I'm really going to help stop it and I've set myself a target − 1,000 signatures (or bust).

Monday
I can't believe it. Some people in this world are just SICK, SICK, SICK. They've signed the petition Mickey Mouse, Sid Vicious and other stupid names. I put all the pictures of the trapped foxes on the noticeboard with it but they just don't care. Anyway, I've counted them up

and I've got 453 proper signatures. God, there's a long way to go. Only one thing for it – I'm going to have to stop people in the street. Scary or what!!!

Sunday

I just kept going – all day yesterday and today. People sometimes make me really mad. Some of them just say 'No' and walk past when you ask them to sign without even knowing what it's about. It seems they don't care about anything. Others are really nice and sign straight away. One man, a soldier, knew all about snaring foxes and thought it was disgusting. He chatted to me for quite a while. It's groups of young people my age that make me die. They laugh at you – not in a horrible way but like they're embarrassed for you. I can see that most of them think I've got guts for doing it. Anyway, I'm nearly there – just a few to go.

June
Monday

Today I sent off my petitions to the RSPCA. It's incredible – 1023 signatures. Surely that will help stop this terrible killing. I wonder if anyone else has got more than me. I don't think so – it was really hard work. I had no idea it would take that long. Anyway – I've done it. CONGRATULATIONS TO ME!

Saturday

What a letdown. I got a standard letter back from the RSPCA today. Three lines, all typed, and it said nothing much. I don't know what I was expecting but at least I thought it would be handwritten. They must know how hard it is to get that many signatures. Okay, okay, I know I did it to save the animals – but all the same . . .

May, 1979
Wednesday
I have just seen the worst thing in my life. I feel sick, disgusted, angry and I want to scream out. I just can't stop thinking about it. I'm writing this now even though it's late because I can't sleep. On the telly were pictures of men killing baby seals on the ice in Canada. They used things like picks with sharp points and smashed them into the heads of the babies. The ice was covered in blood and the worst thing is they were doing it in front of the mothers. You could hear them crying as their babies were killed and skinned. There was one picture of a mother nuzzling the bloody, skinned body of her baby. One killer said the seals were just dollar bills lying on the ice. Anyone who can do this to beautiful, innocent animals is so sick it frightens me. I can't write any more because I feel so helpless and so hopeless.

Saturday
I've been wanting to get my hair cut for so long and today I finally got round to it – really had to push Dad into giving me the money but in the end he did. I really did mean to get it cut but when I got to the precinct an organisation called IFAW (International Fund for Animal Welfare) was giving out info on the seals. They've organised a campaign against the killing. I signed the petition and picked up some leaflets and – hey-ho – I gave them my haircut money! Hairdressing seemed so trivial compared to the awful slaughter. When I got home

Dad asked me why I hadn't had it cut and I told him – I honestly didn't think he'd mind. He went ballistic!!! I don't think I've ever seen him like that before. I just don't understand it. I've really tried to think hard about it and I KNOW if my daughter came home and said she'd given her money to stop the killing of seals I would be proud of her. One of the IFAW leaflets said they are organising a rally next month for the seals. I would really love to go and actually be DOING something.

June
Sunday
Yesterday I travelled from Stockport to London on my own. No one wanted me to go, but I had to do it. It really was a bit scary, not so much the travelling but the rally. I didn't know what to expect. I've seen so many pictures on telly of people rioting and getting hit by police that I was very nervous. As it turned out IT WAS GREAT!!! There were so many people there, shouting, calling and cheering, and so many speakers who said all the things I believe in. I didn't know so many people felt as passionate as I do about animal cruelty. When I arrived someone shoved a banner in my hand which said 'Stop the Bloody Slaughter'. I felt a bit awkward at first – but not for long. I carried it high and shouted and tried to make people listen. For the first time I felt like I was really doing something to stop the cruelty. People all along the road stopped and looked. It was a real high. When it was over I found someone from IFAW and I grabbed hold of them and said I wanted to work for them. I said I would do whatever was necessary and that this was the only thing I want to do now. They were very nice but probably

thought 'stupid girl'. I told Mum when I got back and she said: 'If you want to do it badly enough you will.' Well I do!!!

March, 1980
Tuesday
I'm really looking forward to tomorrow. Lorna's doing a project at sixth form college on farm animals and she's going to a model farm just outside Birmingham – and I'm going with her. It looks like I'll be able to see real animals on a real farm in the countryside. Maybe I'll be able to touch and stroke them. I'll have to say I'm sixteen but everyone thinks I am anyway.

Wednesday
What I have just seen is UNBELIEVABLE!!! I have to try and write it down as I saw it without getting angry. When we arrived I couldn't see a single animal, just huge, great sheds like warehouses. The first one we went in was the pig house. There were about a hundred pigs in the first part and each one was in a concrete and steel pen. They had a collar around their middles and it was attached to the ground with a chain. These poor animals couldn't turn round and could only take a half-step backwards or forwards. They were covered with shit and they stank. This is how they spend most of their life. Even when they give birth it isn't much better – they're still behind metal bars and can hardly move.

I don't think I've ever seen anything so cruel. If people did it to dogs they would be sent to prison. And all the little piglets that had been taken from their mothers were crammed into wire cages, one row on top of another like they were cabbages. But, the thing that got to me most were the boars. Their pens weren't much bigger than the sows, but boars are so huge you can hardly believe it. There were about six of them and the one nearest to me just stood there, his head hanging down. As I got level with him he looked up and dragged himself towards me, limping. I know he did it deliberately — he stared me straight in the eyes and he looked so intelligent but so sad. 'Why are you doing this to me?' I know that's what he was asking me with his eyes. I couldn't answer him and I felt so miserable I burst into tears, and I just kept saying over and over again how sorry I was.

If this is one of the best farms in the country, what must the others be like? I feel sick with shame for the human race and its pathetic excuses. All this cruelty has been taking place all around me and I didn't know about it. I feel ashamed that I didn't know, but now that I do, I can't play a part in this any longer. I must give up meat. I don't know what a vegetarian eats but that's what I'm going to be as from tomorrow.

Friday
She's done it again. She's so unsubtle!! 'Look at this steak, Jules, it's beautiful. Rare, just the way you used to like it.' She knows steak was my favourite. What really pisses me off is the fact that I did want to taste it. But the point is I didn't.

Saturday
Just when I thought it was all over!!! I'm sure there were bits of chopped up chicken in that rice dish. Mum swears there wasn't but I know her better. I think she thinks I'm

going to fade away if I don't eat meat. She is funny. It's become a game with her, seeing if she can slip bits of meat into my food without me knowing. I wonder how often she's been successful? But when I think about it she's been great. She's been really supportive (mostly) and has never really argued with me. I reckon she's now a guilty meat eater, so perhaps I am winning.

July
Monday
Maybe I should be more subtle. Perhaps it wasn't the best thing to push pictures of factory farmed animals under their noses at dinner, telling them that's what they were eating. But I don't understand how they can go on eating it now they know the truth. If I can't persuade my own family, how am I ever going to persuade anyone else?

August
Thursday
We all had to see the careers officer at school today. She asked me what I wanted to do and I said 'save animals'. She laughed. I said I wanted to work with dolphins and stop them being killed. She laughed some more. She asked me to look at a list of jobs which were all boring. I just told her I didn't think she'd been much help and she told me off for being rude. I was only telling the truth. Oh well, that's my career sorted then!!

I talked to my mum today about wanting to work in animal rights. She said if I really wanted it I should follow my heart (even though I know she'd really like me to be a solicitor – YAWN). I know it's the only thing I ever want to do.

*These extracts from May Sarton's first journal show several aspirations emerging. She is determined to go to college, but wants to spend more time working on her writing. She is also fascinated by the theatre and is smitten by the stars that take her 'heart' there. As it turned out she didn't make it to college, but joined a theatre company instead! She later began publishing poetry and novels and, towards the end of her life, published her journals themselves.*

## May Sarton, aged 15

Sunday 5 February, 1928

Well, I have decided to keep a diary after scorning it for so many months. I am afraid it may hurt my poetry, but I have need of expression outside of that. I feel as if my writing at school was getting worse and worse. I am hoping that a diary will cure any self-consciousness. At present what I need most is restraint, a more extensive and careful vocabulary, ease and fluency. I have a long way to go, also enough hope and determination to get me there.

I have started Josephine Preston Peabody's diary and letters as Aunt Agnes advised me. They are wonderful, exquisite 'things'. It encourages me to keep on trying. Why wasn't I born ten years earlier so I could have known some of these people, Amy Lowell amongst others? Well, anyway, I am making brazen strides towards meeting thrilling people that are alive. Friday night I went to *The Jongleur de Notre Dame* with Mary Garden as Jean. She is a great force! I came away surging with admiration for her tremendous vitality and joy in life. There is a donkey in the opera and she very surreptitiously fed him! Isn't that delicious? I had to do something to let off my ardour so I wrote a special delivery to try to get to meet her. I am terrified lest it be sent back and everyone find out, though after all why shouldn't they? Mother would understand. I am a queer person. Here is the letter. I really think it is irresistible! Even if nothing comes of it at least it will have given me the joy and excitement of a real adventure to help me through tomorrow at school; also two or three hours' night-dreaming before I go to sleep.

Dear Mary Garden,

I am pretending that you are not tired yet of being thought exquisite. Friday night I went to the *Jongleur* and came home determined not to write to you although I was bursting with joy and amaze-ment. In vain, however, did I remind myself that I am almost sixteen and should have some sense; in vain did I attempt to convince myself that you wouldn't care anyway. It was impossible. At present I am proud of not having spent a fortune on flowers for you or forcibly burst in and demanded to see you. As for the letter, I assure you it was impossible not to write. The more I think of the *Jongleur* the more I want to see or hear it (what does one say of opera?) again. I am furious because I can't go to *Carmen* again this year! How perfectly delicious it must be to be able to both sing and act so that one can't help writing and telling you how entrancing you are.

I must ask you one question. Did you feed the donkey? I have been arguing about it with my friends since Friday. So you see, you must answer so we won't come to blows! There is no use in my hoping for a chance to see you even for a minute, I suppose. Dreams, especially such heavenly ones, are horrid about coming true. Oh yes, one more thing: I think your French is charming.

> Sincerely, hopefully yours,
> May Sarton

I *was* an ass to put the last in. It spoils the whole thing.

It is a relief to have my thesis on Andrew Jackson done. I am fairly satisfied – I think it is the best that I can do at present. Perhaps it was a little too much influenced by Johnson's *Andrew Jackson*, which I read for reference.

I am very much excited about *Peter Pan*, which a few of the alumni are going to give at Shady Hill. This afternoon I went over to the Clarks' to copy my first scene. I am interested to see what I do with *Pan* as it will be the first time I have done any acting since I decided to seriously aim for theatre. Oh, these ambitions! Why can't I stick to one thing? Well, I can't, so that's that.

## Monday 6 February

This, a Monday, has been comparatively jolly. In the first place I have at last written another poem after about a week of despair. It is not very good but at least it is better than nothing. As long as I can write I can improve, but when there is nothing even to make a start on it is hopeless. School itself didn't seem half so monstrous as usual; I was buoyed up by that blessèd book of JPP's. Tonight I am going to see the fancy skating contests at the rink. I am looking forward to it eagerly. The smooth rhythm of beautiful skating literally makes me feel as if my heart were in my mouth. I am almost sick with the sheer curve of bodies.

How long will it take before my writing is like a snow-flake — clear, and frosty and fine-wrought? Well, I have inordinate hope so courage, heart!

## Tuesday 7 February

When something beautiful makes a hush in my heart, tears come to my eyes and I catch my breath. When I see a friend sad, or when I am very angry, I cry. But I cannot understand how I can cry at a failure which is my own fault. This term I got D (almost fail) in Latin; F (fail) in Algebra; G (good) in English; E (excellent) in History. I must buckle down to work. It will mean less reading and less time for writing or thinking, but I have set out for college and now I have got to see it through. When will they finish educating me? The aching part of it is that I don't believe it is worthwhile. I feel all the time as if I were wasting time, time so terribly precious.

When I came home from school I quietly ate lunch and talked with Mother without realising what bliss waited for me on the table — a letter back from Mary Garden! She must have written as soon as she received mine! It is so delightful, more so than my dearest hope.

Dear Miss Sarton,

A thousand thanks for your most charming letter — I *am* so glad you enjoyed 'The Juggler' — I think it is divine — Yes, I gave the donkey bits of sugar — for I wanted him to love me — you know animals don't differ much from human beings, do they?

With my best regards and greetings!

She has huge, windy writing full of life and love of life. I think she must be heavenly. Mary Garden, you have my heart! Like the donkey your piece of sugar has filled my soul with longing for more. (Talk about sentimentality!) Why oh why can't I got to *Carmen*? I said I would give up hope tonight but I can't. Isn't there a possibility of my finding ten dollars tomorrow on the street, or a pot of gold in the yard? I simply must get famous so I can meet some of these people. I think it is a great pity that I don't live in an aristocratic country. I seem to be one of those primitive types of people who need somebody to adore. Funny child that I am! I wonder if I shall still amuse myself in my old age by writing to famous actresses and opera singers and poets.

Tuesday over! Only three days before a little oasis of Saturday and Sunday. One more day in the eternity of life. One more day towards growing up.

Wednesday 8 February

I am breathing in and trying to make part of me that singing heart of JPP's. I read it in small doses to be sure to appreciate it all. I feel now as if I had a beautiful garden, quite wild in places, but all softened down by twilight to go to when I want peace, and a forget-me-not to stick in my heart's button-hole for inspiration.

*Carmen* is over and I couldn't hear it! Next year seems so terribly far away! I am going to begin saving now so I can get at least one orchestra seat. Miss Sullivan (my English teacher) seems quite excited about the poetry contest. She met one of the judges at Harvard yesterday who said that there were floods of poetry coming in. I believe she really thinks I have some chance. It is a pity, because I know I haven't. I am going to try to get some poetry published so I may have a little extra money. I think I'll attack the *Atlantic* (to begin high) when my poems are sent back from *Poetry*. I went into the Coop bookstore to buy this diary and of course spent a few moments of longing in the book department. In April I think I can afford JPP's complete poetical works.

## Saturday 11 February

I forgot to say anything about the concert on Thursday. It has left a little well of joy in my heart that I can go back to re-quaff every now and then. It was beautiful, beautiful, beautiful, and still beautiful, and more beautiful. They played three things – Mozart's Symphony in E flat major, Strauss's *Don Juan* and the Sibelius 1st Symphony in E minor. The Mozart, which I had not expected to like very much, was like a fresh breeze. The exquisite symmetry of it delighted me. *Don Juan* I didn't like, perhaps partly because Sanders Theatre is too small for such noisy music. But it is Sibelius that lifted me up into heaven. It seemed strangely familiar as if I had somewhere heard it in a far dream beyond a blue threshold. I always seemed to know what was coming and yet when it did come it was as if I had not known. The greatest wave swept over me, leaving me half blind and dumb with song, half crazy with sound.

## Sunday 12 February

I'm off chasing a star again! Jean T wrote a letter to Katherine Warren, the chief actress of the Rep, and got a heavenly letter back asking her to go to see her and talk about acting. The letter was six pages long, and she called it brief! I immediately rushed home and wrote a special delivery, which I shall copy when I find it. In the letter to Jean she asked her to call her up and today Jean did. Her (KW's) mother answered the phone, but made an appointment for Tuesday, and I'm to go too. She had evidently got my letter! Really I have too much luck. I just have to wish a thing and I get it! Never again will I say that dreams don't come true. Here is the letter I wrote:

Dear Katherine Warren,

Jean Tatlock having gotten (how could I make such a mistake, I only thought of it when the letter was mailed) your letter is in heaven and I am on the edge out of sheer joy that such a great dream could come true! I have kept this letter, at least the last part of it, for a week because I am trying to be more controlled. I am much too emotional, but this is off the point which I shall blunder out in a minute. Why can't I send you a snow-flake, clear and frosty and fine wrought, instead of words and words.

Ibsen at present makes me burn to act – Hedda Gabler, Hilda Wangel, Nora, Rebecca West – but especially Hedda Gabler. There is no reason for my telling you that you were exquisite, almost hurtingly beautiful, as Hedda Gabler, but I will tell you it. The only thing I can send you that will not be self-conscious is a poem I wrote. It is poor, but I feel as if it were the nearest thing to a snow-flake I have to

give you. (Then I copied my 'Hedda Gabler' poem).
It lacks restraint and precision. (I can't remember
what came next).

Mayn't I come to see you and ask one or two
questions about acting? I am going away this
Thursday for a week dash it all! But please O please
write or just send a postcard with yes on it if I may
before then. That is what the impetuous part of me
is singing but my sensible part says, very shocked,
'People don't do such things!' I am going to pretend
they do – by special delivery!

Hopefully.

I have spent the day chiefly doing homework and reading
GK Chesterton. He surely is clever, sometimes too clever,
but still stimulating. Now for a poem – Hurrah!

# Travel

*A good way to practise writing skills is by writing about travel — 'travel writing' — recording places and events which are new to you, and so much more interesting than normal, everyday life!*

*In this letter to her friend Fanny Imlay, Mary Wollstonecraft Shelley writes of the dramatic scenery she passed through to reach Lake Geneva in Switzerland. This letter was to be published, with others by Mary and Percy Bysshe Shelley, in* Journal of a Six Weeks' Tour. *Two years later, in Geneva again, Mary was to begin her famous classic* Frankenstein *— and the wild and compelling descriptions in this letter give us a taste of what was to follow!*

## Mary Wollstonecraft Shelley, aged 19

Hôtel de Sécheron, Geneva
17 May, 1816

To Fanny

We arrived at Paris on the 8th of this month, and were detained two days for the purpose of obtaining the various signatures necessary to our passports, the French government having become much more circumspect since the escape of Lavalette [*French politician, condemned to death by Louis VIII*]. We had no letters of introduction, or any friend in that city, and were therefore confined to our hotel, where we were obliged to hire apartments for the week, although when we first arrived we expected to be detained one night only; for in Paris there are no houses where you can be accommodated with apartments by the day.

The manners of the French are interesting, although

less attractive, at least to Englishmen, than before the last invasion of the Allies: the discontent and sullenness of their minds perpetually betrays itself. Nor is it wonderful that they should regard the subjects of a government which fills their country with hostile garrisons, and sustains a detested dynasty on the throne, with an acrimony and indignation of which that government alone is the proper object. This feeling is honourable to the French, and encouraging to all those of every nation in Europe who have a fellow feeling with the oppressed, and who cherish an unconquerable hope that the cause of liberty must at length prevail.

Our route after Paris, as far as Troyes, lay through the same uninteresting tract of country which we had traversed on foot nearly two years before, but on quitting Troyes we left the road leading to Neufchâtel, to follow that which was to conduct us to Geneva. We entered Dijon on the third evening after our departure from Paris, and passing through Dôle, arrived at Poligny. This town is built at the foot of Jura, which rises abruptly from a plain of vast extent. The rocks of the mountain overhang the houses. Some difficulty in procuring horses detained us here until the evening closed in, when we proceeded, by the light of a stormy moon, to Champagnolles, a little village situated in the depth of the mountains. The road was serpentine and exceedingly steep, and was overhung on one side by half distinguished precipices, whilst the other was a gulph, filled by the darkness of the driving clouds. The dashing of the invisible mountain streams announced to us that we had quitted the plains of France, as we slowly ascended, amidst a violent storm of wind and rain, to Champagnolles, where we arrived at twelve o'clock, the fourth night after our departure from Paris.

The next morning we proceeded, still ascending among the ravines and vallies of the mountain. The scenery perpetually grows more wonderful and sublime: pine forests of impenetrable thickness, and untrodden, nay, inaccessible expanse spread on every side. Sometimes the dark woods descending, follow the route into the vallies, the distorted trees struggling with knotted roots between the most barren clefts; sometimes the road winds high into the regions of frost, and then the forests become scattered, and the branches of the trees are loaded with snow, and half of the enormous pines themselves buried in the wavy drifts. The spring, as the inhabitants informed us, was unusually late, and indeed the cold was excessive; as we ascended the mountains, the same clouds which rained on us in the vallies poured forth large flakes of snow thick and fast. The sun occasionally shone through these showers, and illuminated the magnificent ravines of the mountains, whose gigantic pines were some laden with snow, some wreathed round by the lines of scattered and lingering vapour; others darting their dark spires into the sunny sky, brilliantly clear and azure.

As the evening advanced, and we ascended higher, the snow, which we had beheld whitening the overhanging rocks, now encroached upon our road, and it snowed fast as we entered the village of Les Rousses, where we were threatened by the apparent necessity of passing the night in a bad inn and dirty beds. For from that place there are two roads to Geneva; one by Nion, in the Swiss territory, where the mountain route is shorter, and comparatively easy at that time of the year, when the road is for several leagues covered with snow of an enormous depth; the other road lay through Gex, and was too circuitous and dangerous to be attempted at so late an hour in the day. Our passport, however, was for Gex, and we were told that we could not change its destination; but all these police laws, so severe in themselves, are to be softened by bribery, and this difficulty was at length overcome. We hired four horses, and ten men to support the carriage, and departed from Les Rousses at six in the evening, when the sun had already far descended, and the snow pelting against the windows of our carriage, assisted the coming darkness to deprive us of the view of the lake of Geneva and the far-distant Alps.

The prospect around, however, was sufficiently sublime to command our attention – never was scene more awfully desolate. The trees in these regions are incredibly large, and stand in scattered clumps over the white wilderness; the vast expanse of snow was chequered only by these gigantic pines, and the poles that marked our road: no river or rock-encircled lawn relieved the eye, by adding the picturesque to the sublime. The natural silence of that uninhabited desert contrasted strangely with the voices of the men who conducted us, who, with animated tones and gestures, called to one another in a patois composed of French and Italian, creating disturbance where, but for them, there was none.

To what a different scene are we now arrived! To the warm sunshine and to the humming of sun-loving insects. From the windows of our hotel we see the lovely lake, blue as the heavens which it reflects, and sparkling with golden beams. The opposite shore is sloping and covered with vines, which however do not so early in the season add to the beauty of the prospect. Gentlemen's seats are scattered over these banks, behind which rise the various ridges of black mountains, and towering far above, in the midst of its snowy Alps, the majestic Mont Blanc, highest and queen of all. Such is the view reflected by the lake; it is a bright summer scene without any of that sacred solitude and deep seclusion that delighted us at Lucerne.

We have not yet found out any very agreeable walks, but you know our attachment to water excursions. We have hired a boat, and every evening at about six o'clock we sail on the lake, which is delightful, whether we glide over a glassy surface or are speeded along by a strong wind. The waves of this lake never afflict me with that sickness that deprives me of all enjoyment in a sea voyage; on the contrary, the tossing of our boat raises my spirits and inspires me with unusual hilarity. Twilight here is of short duration, but we at present enjoy the benefit of an increasing moon, and seldom return until ten o'clock, when, as we approach the shore, we are saluted by the delightful scent of flowers and new mown grass, and the chirp of the grasshoppers, and the song of the evening birds.

We do not enter into society here, yet our time passes swiftly and delightfully. We read Latin and Italian during the heats of noon, and when the sun declines we walk in the garden of the hotel, looking at the rabbits, relieving fallen cockchaffers, and watching the motions of a myriad of lizards, who inhabit a southern wall of the garden. You know that we have just escaped from the gloom of winter and of London; and coming to this delightful spot during this divine weather, I feel as happy as a new-fledged bird, and hardly care what twig I fly to, so that I may try my new-found wings. A more experienced bird may be more difficult in its choice of a bower; but, in my present temper of mind, the budding flowers, the fresh grass of spring, and the happy creatures about me that live and enjoy these pleasures, are quite enough to afford me exquisite delight, even though clouds should shut out Mont Blanc from my sight. Adieu!

*Virginia Woolf began a diary at the age of fifteen, recording her busy daily life in London. After a pause of a few years she started again while on holiday in Cambridgeshire, this time with the aim of practising her writing style. The results, shown in the extracts to follow are some beautiful and evocative descriptions of the Cambridgeshire fens.*

## Virginia Woolf, aged 19

12 August, 1899

Adrian & I have a habit now when the days are so hot, of keeping our exercise till after tea, & then of going out on our bicycles for an hour's hard riding. Besides picturesque advantages, this country possesses the solid one that all its main roads are excellently made, well hammered, smooth & free from stray stones. This country, too, does not hamper the cyclist by any disturbing Hills; you may ride & ride & ride without ever being forced to dismount & push yr. bicycle up a hill, or without ever having the delight of raising yr. feet & spinning downhill. This evening we went along the road which crosses the railway at the station by a Bridge & then runs as straight as a yard measure for a good four miles. These roads have their beauties to the eye of a Fen lover, but a Bicyclist is a mechanical animal. Not until we dismounted did we appreciate the scenery. On both sides it was dead flat – the road was slightly raised in the middle & runs through the plain like a straight white thread. This is the midst of the old Fen country. This solid ground on which we stood was, not many years ago, all swamp & reed; now indeed there is a pathway, & on either side grow potatoes & corn, but the Fen character remains indelible. A broad ditch crosses the Fen, in which there is cold brown water even in this hot summer. Tall rushes & water plants grow from it; & small white moths, the inhabitants of the Fens, were fluttering among them in scores when we were there. I wish that once & for all I could put down in this wretched handwriting how this country impresses me – how great I feel the stony-hard flatness & monotony of the plain. Every time I write in this book I find myself drifting into the attractive but impossible task of describing the Fens – till I grow heartily sick of so much feeble word painting; & long for one expressive quotation that should signify in its solitary compass all the glories of earth air & Heaven. Nevertheless I own it is a joy to me to be set down with such a vast never ending picture to reproduce – reproduction is out of the question – but to gaze at, nibble at & scratch at.

After all we are a world of imitations; all the Arts that is to say imitate as far as they can the one great truth that all can see. Such is the eternal instinct in the human beast, to try & reproduce something of that majesty in paint marble or ink. Somehow ink tonight seems to me the least effectual method of all – & music the nearest to truth.

3 September *A Chapter on Sunsets*

A showery day with wind & watery clouds is excellent material for a sunset. A day of unclouded majesty, heat & serenity has a sunset of extraordinary magnificence of light so unapproachable by pen or paint that the author & artist prefer for the sake of their art the more attainable forms of cloud which can be likened by an imaginative person to castles & hills & rocky towns that have their counterpart on earth.

No one – save a poet – can express in words or paint the human significance & pathos of the sun's unclouded rain of light – that makes the Heavens a delight & a difficulty to look upon. This land, as I have had occasion to remark before, is a land whose chief attraction is its sky. It is as if you were slung on a flat green board in mid air; with only sky sky sky around & above & beneath you. In this way alone I think that the Fen country deserves to be called one of the most beautiful countries in England. We have this moment come in from a sunset expedition – an account of which I must at once write down, or I shall never attempt it. Nothing methinks is so impossible as to describe a real sunset in pen & ink three days after that sunset has faded from the sky.

To begin then. Today has been windy stormy & raining – too great an abundance of water indeed to make a really grand sunset.

[*Today*] at 6.30 we started along the Huntingdon road, & the sun [*was*] then just entering the cloud belt on the Horizon. It sank so [*slow*]ly that we, who reproached G[*eorge*] for having brought us out [*so*] early, found ourselves in a minute in the midst of the performance.

[*So*] quickly did the clouds catch the glory, glow, & fade, that our eyes & mind had ample work merely to register the change. The main features were three; a red ball of a sun, first; then a low lying bank of grey cloud, whose upper edges were already feathery & fixed to receive into its arms the impetuous descent of the sun god; thirdly, a group of trees which made our horizon; casting their arms against the sky; then fourthly, a cloud shaped like an angel's wing, so − [*drawing*] The edge of this was [*two illegible words*] with fire − vivid & glowing in the east like some sword of judgement or vengeance − & yet the intensity of its light melted & faded as it touched the grey sky behind; so that there was no clearly defined outline. This is one observation that I have made from my observation of many sunsets − that no shape of cloud has one line in it in the least sharp or hard − nowhere can you draw a straight line with your pencil & say 'This line goes so'. Everything is done by different shades & degrees of light − melting & mixing infinitely − Well may an Artist despair!

This was the central point of the sunset − but when our eyes found an instant to leave it there was another glory, reflected indeed but no less glorious & perfect of its kind than the original, all round. The afternoon had scattered grey clouds pall mall about the sky. Some of these were now conglomerated into one vast cloud field in the east & south − others were sailing like solitary icebergs. All bore on their way the imprint: the dying kiss − of the sun. The icebergs shone glowing pale crimson; the ice fields were broken up into exquisite blocks of crimson lint − a crimson which looked all the more delicate & exquisite that it is besprinkled with soft cold grey.

This was all over in ten minutes – when we got back home the east & west were rapidly taking on the darkness of night. No gleams of crimson lived to tell that the sun had sunk.

Wednesday evening, 20 September

The day has come at last of which I have thought so much. It is my habit, on this the last page of the book, to sum up my judgement & deliver my verdict on the summer entire. But I feel that I have left unexpressed one phase of the summer, the last autumnal phase which, before I reach London, I want to write down.

Briefly then a change has come over the country since I last wrote. Then it was summer; now it is autumn. I drove back alone from St Ives on Monday, & felt the change each step of the five miles. Where the corn stood yellow & luxuriant, there are now fields of brown clods, which leave a decided impression on one's eyes when one sees the country spread beneath one. The still days of haze & blue distance are over; a sharp wind comes racing over the plain, & brown coveys of partridges rise from the stubble that yet stands. The summer wealth of cultivation is over; & the earth is preparing for her time of sleep & slow reproduction. The hedges all along the roads are laden with scarlet berries, which if nature shows in this liberality her intention of inflicting on bird & man a hard winter foretell months of ice & snow. The little brown birds rise in a cloud & go twittering high up in the air over the brown fields. There is that mellow clearness in the air, which softens & matures the land & the men's faces who till it. There is a look & feeling of melancholy in everything – that melancholy which is the sweetest tongue of thought.

'The woods decay – the woods decay & fall –
The vapours weep their burden to the ground'

This – if it be legitimate quotation – expresses the next stage of autumn. At the present moment the change from summer is more exquisite; though as delicious as winter. Brown & ruddy colours have stolen across what was green & gold; a thousand delicate vivid hues have supplanted the prevailing luxuriant green in hedge & grass & leaf & plant. But for me the definite touch that has spelt autumn is the subtle difference in the air. It brings with it odours of burning wood & weeds; & delicious moisture from the shaven earth; it is cleaner & more virile; it is autumn in its youth, before decayed woods & weeping vapours have come to end its substance. We saw, what I always love to see when we bicycled to Ramsey (for the last time) on Saturday, weed burning on the hill. Look at the picture of Sir John Millais of children burning leaves & my theories will be revealed. I cannot attempt to explain in words the charm & melancholy, the colour & the interest, of the picture. We thought the hedge was burning; the wind blew the flames so high & such a distance. At moments there was only a smouldering white smoke, & then of a sudden the flames leapt out & lashed their tongues.

Well, the time has come to have done with Autumn & with everything else. I have spent the evening packing our Red box for its return journey; & now my room is swept bare of books & everything save what I carry in my own bag.

Tomorrow at this hour I shall be in my room in London! The roar of the city will be booming in my ear, which seven weeks of Warboys will have made as sensitive as any country cousin's. I write this down to see if it looks any more credible in pen & ink; but I cannot bring my mind to bear upon the change. I know that we are going on a journey tomorrow, but I cannot realise, though I repeat it to myself all day long, that the journey will end in London —

I add this last of last words in a moment which I have stolen before consigning this work to my bag. I am packing my own precious Goods which are the last to be packed & the first to be unpacked.

Well then farewell Warboys. The summer ranks among our happiest I think; & this land of plain & sky will remain a distinct & lovely picture in my mind were I never to see it again.

Goodbye to Fens & flat fields & windmills & sky domes.

Farewell Manchester
Noble Town, Farewell.
Thursday Morning
September 21st      a swan's song

# Friends

*Where would we be without our friends to share the good times and the bad? Although sometimes it seems friends can be very cruel too!*

*In these extracts from Yvonne Coppard's diary, among the ordinary daily problems of sisters, teachers and boyfriends, we see Yvonne and a long-term friend, Mog (aka Susan), fall out with a more recent arrival on the scene, Lorry (aka Lorraine). However, as is often the case with best friends, it doesn't last for long . . . (and Brian, if you're reading this, she's sorry!)*

## Yvonne Coppard, aged 14–15

Thursday 2 January, 1969
Today I settled to a monumental task – improving my memory. It's the only New Year resolution I've made. (I might forget the others, ho ho.) Every time I put something down or move an object etc., I concentrate on remembering its exact position. Don't think it will last long – worth a try.

Went round to Susan's this evening. We went down the chip shop and then she set my hair in heated rollers and stuff (she got them for Christmas). It took FOREVER and my hair didn't look any different to me, but I pretended I was really pleased.

Monday 6 January
Back to school. EUUGH! Double Maths with Baxter AND French. Euugh, euugh! Just about managed to stay out of trouble, though. At least we didn't get any homework.

59

Sunday 12 January
MY BIRFDY
Got mostly money, plus tights, slip, make-up, pencil case and hankies (I don't think Dad knows tissues have been invented). Was supposed to be going to the pictures with Lorry and Mog and Caroline, but we didn't fancy it – too cold and wet. So we stayed over at Mog's and raided her mum's old make-up (her mum knew we were doing it, but not about the new eyeliner from the other make-up bag). Had a good laugh. Got home at midnight – too tired to wash it all off. Probably get all spotty now.

Friday 24 January
Left my bag on the bus – again! It had my Geography book in it. Phoned Lost Property – they haven't got it. Jones will go nuts. He thinks I do it deliberately, just because this is the third time in a couple of months that I've lost it. My life won't be worth it if I don't get it back before he finds out.

Had Games – hockey. Lovely – scored a goal. Went to Youth Club. It was BORING. Why do I go?

Sunday 2 February
Mog and I had a row with Lorry. It was our fault really. We said some stuff we shouldn't have. Lorry took the huff and made some really bitchy remarks about us. Caroline was there too. I'm not sure if she's at loggerheads too. Lorry was really sarcastic. It hurt. I don't want to write any more than that.

Monday 3 February
Jones discovered the Awful Truth about my book. He

has put me in lunchtime detention every day until I've copied up all the notes, and I have to pay for the new exercise book. He was so cross I thought he'd blow up. He's not exactly going to be sparkling company every lunchtime.

Caroline is still friends. Lorry is definite foe. Caroline says she was being really nasty about me and Mog. Last night I felt bad and wanted to make up. Now I feel more like slapping her face!

Saturday 8 February
Went to a dance at St Nick's. Got a new skirt, new top and took Cathy's cardigan. I hope she doesn't notice before I get a chance to put it back! Met Brian – nice looking, seventeen, all right. He asked me to go out with him next week. To a football match! I said yes, though. You never know. I might even end up a fan.

Monday 10 February
Saw Lorry at Youth Club. She ignored me, I ignored her. Mog couldn't go. Had to play table tennis all night with Gill. Felt rotten. Maybe won't go again.

Saturday 15 February
Met Brian at Eastcote Station. Went by tube to Shepherd's Bush – got to the football place two hours early! Brian told me you had to, to get a good place. He didn't tell me the match didn't start until three o'clock, or that we'd have to stand up all the time. By the time the match finished we'd stood there four hours. There were loads and loads of people – the bloke behind kept swearing, and one man told him to belt up because there

61

was 'a little girl' in front of him. Bloody cheek!

We walked through Shepherd's Bush Market afterwards. There were police on horses, and more people than I've ever seen in one place. George Best was playing, and I'm glad I saw him in real life, but the match was one of the most boring things that have ever happened to me and Brian is not wonderful enough to be compensation for that. (He kept talking about it afterwards, as well. I just wanted to get home.) Brian asked me out for tomorrow. I said yes, but I'm not sure this is going anywhere. We're going bowling. Maybe I should give him a chance to prove he does know how to go out with a girl properly.

Sunday 16 February
Was supposed to meet Brian in Northwood Hills at seven o'clock. Wanted to borrow Cathy's skirt but she was in, so I had to ask. She said no. I didn't go to meet Brian – couldn't be bothered. Hope he didn't wait long – wanted to phone him, but we forgot to tell each other numbers! Went to the pictures in Ruislip with Lorry and Mog instead. At least we're all friends again.

*Like the characters in her novels,* Jane Eyre, Shirley *and* Villette, *Charlotte Brontë had to work as a school teacher (or governess) – it being the only respectable way for a middle-class woman to earn a living in the nineteenth century. Unlike her fictional characters, Charlotte had two very good friends to help her through the bad times – Ellen Nussey and Mary Taylor. Only the letters to Ellen have survived, and in these we see Charlotte confiding her utter despair of teaching, but also her love for her dear friend.*

## Charlotte Brontë, aged 19–20

Haworth
2 July, 1835

Dear Ellen

I had hoped to have had the extreme pleasure of seeing you at Haworth this summer, but human affairs are mutable, and human resolutions must bend to the course of events – We are all about to divide, break up, separate; Emily is going to school, Branwell is going to London, and I am going to be a Governess. This last determination I formed myself, knowing that I should have to take the step sometime, and 'better sune as syne' to use the Scotch proverb and knowing also that Papa would have enough to do with his limited income should Branwell be placed at the Royal Academy, and Emily at Roe-Head. Where am I going to reside? you will ask – within four miles of Yourself dearest at a place neither of us are wholly unacquainted with, being no other than the identical Roe-Head mentioned above. Yes I am going to teach, in the very school where I was myself taught – Miss Wooler made me the offer and I preferred it to one or two proposals of Private Governesship which I had before received – I am sad, very sad at the thoughts of leaving home but Duty – Necessity – these are stern Mistresses who will not be disobeyed. Did I not once say Ellen you ought to be thankful for your independence? I felt what I said at the time, and I repeat it now with double earnestness: if any thing would cheer me, it is the idea of being so near you – surely you and Polly will come, and see me – it would be wrong in me to doubt it – you were never unkind yet. Emily, and I leave home on the 29th of this month, the idea of being together consoles us both somewhat – and in truth since I must enter a situation 'my lines have fallen in pleasant places' – I both love, and respect Miss Wooler – What did you mean Ellen by saying that you knew the reason why I wished to have a letter from your sister Mercy? the sentence hurt me though I did not quite understand it. My *only* reason was a desire to correspond with a person I have a regard for; give my love both to her and to Sarah and Miss Nussey, remember me respectfully to Mrs Nussey, and believe me my dearest friend

Affectionately, warmly Yours
C Brontë

My paper has I see got somehow disgracefully blotted, but as I really have not time to write another letter, I must beg you to excuse its slovenly appearance – pray let no one else see it – for the writing into the bargain is shameful.

Roe Head
26 September, 1836

Last Saturday afternoon being in one of my sentimental humours I sat down and wrote to you such a note as I ought to have written to none but M Taylor who is nearly as mad as myself; today when I glanced it over it occurred to me that Ellen's calm eye would look at this with scorn, so I determined to concoct some production more fit for the inspection of common Sense. I will not tell you all I think, and feel about you Ellen. I will preserve unbroken that reserve which alone enables me to maintain a decent character for judgement; but for that I should long ago have been set down by all who know me as a Frenchified – fool. You have been very kind to me of late, and gentle and you have spared me those little sallies of ridicule which owing to my miserable and wretched touchiness of character used formerly to make me wince as if I had been touched with a hot iron: things that nobody else cares for enter into my mind and rankle there like venom. I know these feelings are absurd and therefore I try to hide them but they only sting the deeper for concealment. I'm an idiot! –

I was informed that your brother George was at Mirfield church last Sunday. Of course I did not *see* him though I guessed his presence because I heard his cough (my short–sightedness makes my ear very acute). Miss Uptons told me he was there: they were quite smitten; he was the sole subject of their conversation during the whole of the subsequent evening. Miss Eliza described to me every part of his dress and likewise that of a gentleman who accompanied him with astonishing minuteness. I laughed most heartily at her graphic details, and so would you if you had been with me.

Ellen I wish I could live with you always, I begin to cling to you more fondly than ever I did. If we had but a cottage and a competency of our own I do think we might live and love on till *Death* without being dependent on any third person for happiness.

Farewell my own dear Ellen
[Unsigned]

October, 1836
[?]Roe Head

Weary with a day's had work – during which an unusual degree of Stupidity has been displayed by my promising pupils I am sitting down to write a few hurried lines to my dear Ellen. Excuse me if I say nothing but nonsense, for my mind is exhausted, and dispirited. It is a Stormy evening and the wind is uttering a continual moaning sound that makes me feel very melancholy – At such times, in such moods as these Ellen it is my nature to seek repose in some calm, tranquil idea and I have now summoned up your image to give me rest. There you sit, upright and still in your black dress and white scarf – your pale, marble-like face – looking so serene and kind – just like reality – I wish you would speak to me. If we should be separated, if it should be our lot to live at a great distance and never to see each other again, in old age how I should call up the memory of my youthful days and what a melancholy pleasure I should feel in dwelling on the recollection of my Early Friend Ellen Nussey!

If I like people it is my nature to tell them so and I am not afraid of offering incense to your vanity. It is from religion that you derive your chief charm and may its influence always preserve you as pure, as unassuming and as benevolent in thought and deed as you are now. What am I compared to you? I feel my own utter worthlessness when I make the comparison. I'm a very coarse, common-place wretch!

Ellen, I have some qualities that make me very miserable, some feelings that you can have no participation in – that few very few people in the world can at all understand. I don't pride myself on these peculiarities, I strive to conceal and suppress them as much as I can, but they burst out sometimes and then those who see the explosion despise me and I hate myself for days afterwards. We are going to have prayers so I can write no more of this trash yet it is too true.

I must send this note for want of a better. I don't know what to say. I've just received your epistle and what accompanied it, I can't tell what should induce your Sisters to waste their kindness on such a one as me. I'm obliged to them and I hope you'll tell them so – I'm obliged to you also, more for your note than for your present; the first gave me pleasure, the last something very like pain. Give my love to both your Sisters and my thanks; the bonnet is too handsome for me. I dare write no more. When shall we meet again?

C Brontë

*These passionate letters by Katherine Mansfield show her developing friendship with Sylvia Payne over four years – from when they were at school together to Katherine's move to New Zealand. Katherine frequently points out they are much better friends by post than they ever were in person – so they were true penfriends indeed! In 1907 Katherine did have some stories published in a magazine, so she was already well on her way to achieving her aims . . .*

## Katherine Mansfield, aged 15–19

The Retreat, Bexley, Kent
23 December, 1903

Dearest Sylvia

I want to write to you this afternoon, so here I am – I am not at all surprised at myself, I knew that I would not wait till you had written. Why should we lose any time in knowing each other when we have lost so much already.

I cannot tell you how sorry I am that I shall not see you again. I like you much more than any other girl I have met in England & I seem to see less of you. We just stand upon the threshold of each other's heart and never get right in. What I mean by 'heart' is just this. My heart is a place where everything I love (whether it be in imagination or in truth) has a free entrance. It is where I store my memories, all my happiness and my sorrow and there is a large compartment in it labelled '*Dreams*'. There are many many people that I like very much, but they generally view my public rooms, and they call me false, and mad, and changeable. I would not show them what I was really like for worlds. They would think me madder I suppose –

I wish we could know each other, so that I might be able to say 'Sylvia is one of my *best* friends.' Don't think that I mean half I look and say to other people. I cannot think why I so seldom am myself. I think I rather hug myself to myself, too much. Don't you? Not that it is beautiful or precious. It is a very shapeless, bare, undecorated thing just yet. I have been fearfully cross this morning – It was about my music. Yesterday I got a concerto from Tom for a Xmas present and I tryed it over with Vera this morning. She

68

*counted aloud* and said *wrong wrong*, called me a pig, and then said she would go and tell Aunt Louie I was swearing at her. I laugh as I read this now. At the time I felt *ill* with anger. So much for my excellent temper!!

It is quiet here now. I am alone in my bedroom. O don't you just thank God for quiet? I do. If only it could last though. Something always disturbs it. There is a bird somewhere outside crying          , yet for all this, I am sorry, very sorry, to have left London. I like it so very much. Next term I really shall work hard. I MUST – I am so fearfully idle & conceited.

Why I have written this letter, I do not know. Forgive me dear. I do not dare to read it through. I should burn it if I did. Goodbye for the present. I beg of you write soon to

> Your very loving Friend
> Kathleen

[*On back of last page*]
> Private.
> If you feel absurd or jolly don't read this.
> Private.

> [*Queen's College*] 41 Harley Street W.
> 24 January, 1904

Dearest Sylvia –

It was ripping of you to write to me such a long letter! I was very pleased to receive it. I certainly do *hate* fogs. They are abominable. Yesterday I did nothing but practise and I wrote to Gladys and to Tom. I heard from G. yesterday morning. It was a perfectly lovely letter, but *so* queer. Just exactly like her. I do wish that people did not think her fast, or empty. She has more in her than almost anyone else I know. She has the most glorious ideas about things, and is wonderfully clever – Her letters are just full of keen originality, and *power*. Do you understand? Perhaps other people would think them foolish. I don't. O, how thankful I am to be back at College, but, Sylvia, I am *ashamed* at the way in which I long for German. I simply can't help it. It is dreadful. And when I go into class, I feel I must just stare at him the whole time. I never liked anyone so much. Every day I like him more. Yet on Thursday he was like *ice*! By the way, is not this *heavenly*: – 'To every man, there come noble thoughts which flash across his heart like great white birds.' (Maeterlinck.)

O, that is wonderful. Great white birds. Is not that perfect?! I wish there was not a night before College. O, I wish you were a boarder!!! What times we would have together. I do love you so, much more each time I see you. So little goes on here. All the girls are so very dull.

On Friday afternoon I went to Mudie's. What a fascinating place it is!! I had some peeps into most lovely books, & the *bindings* were exquisite. I always think that it is so sinful to publish 'Bloody Hands', by Augusta St John, in green leather, & *Bleak House* in paper for 6d. '*Tout marche de travers* [*Everything goes wrong*].' That is very true!

My writing this afternoon is most erratic. I do not know why. You know you always say that you are not *17*, well, pardon me, I think you *are quite*. I mean to *work* specially hard, this term. I am taking *19* hours. Dear, I must finish this 'ego'. You must be tired of it

With my love from<br>
Your loving Friend<br>
Kathleen

30 Manchester Street, W.
24 April, 1906

My dearest Cousin,

I was so delighted to get your letter yesterday — and to hear what a fine time you are having. Truth to tell — I am just longing for the country — and especially for pine woods — they have a mystical fascination for me — but all trees have. Woods and the sea — both are perfect.

We have been staying here since last Friday with Father and Mother, and have had a very good time. I don't think I have ever laughed more. They are both just the same *and* we leave for New Zealand in October. Strange thought — for some things I am very glad, now — but I feel as though all my English life was over, already. Do you know — I have a fancy that when I am there, we shall write far more often and know each other far better than we do now. I do hope it will be so — dear — because I have always wanted us to be friends — and we never seem to pass a certain point — once a Term, perhaps, I feel 'Sylvia & I really know each other now', and next time we meet — the feeling is gone.

A great change has come into my life since I saw you last. Father is greatly opposed to my wish to be a professional 'cellist or to take up the 'cello to any great extent — so my hope for a musical career is absolutely gone. It was a fearful disappointment — I could not tell you what I have felt like — and do now when I think of it — but I suppose it is no earthly use warring with the Inevitable — so in the future I shall give *all* my time to writing. There are great opportunities for a girl in New Zealand — she has so much time and quiet — and we have an ideal little 'cottage by the sea' where I mean to spend a good deal of my time. Do you *love* solitude as I do – especially if I am in a writing mood – and will you do so – too. Write, I mean, in the Future. I feel sure that you would be splendidly successful –

I am so keen upon all women having a *definite* future – are not you? The idea of sitting still and waiting for a husband is absolutely revolting – and it really is the attitude of a great many girls. Do you know I have read none of the books that you mentioned. Is not that shocking – but – Sylvia – you know that little 'Harold Brown' shop in Wimpole Shop [*for Street*] – I picked up a small collection of poems entitled *The Silver Net* by Louis Vintras – and I liked some of them immensely. The atmosphere is so *intense*. He seems to me to belong to that school which flourished just a few years ago – but which now has not a single representative – a kind of impressionist literature school. Don't think that I even approve of them – but they interest me – Dowson – Sherard – School. It rather made me smile to read of you wishing you could create your fate – O, how many times I have felt just the same. I just long for power over circumstances – & always feel as though I could do such a great deal more good than is done – & give such a lot of pleasure – *aber* [*but*] . . .

We have not seen a great deal of the Bakers, but they are flourishing. Mother asks me if you know a house suitable for a lady, two wee children and two maids anywhere near? It is just by the way. I am enjoying this Hotel life. There is a kind of feeling of irresponsibility about it that is fascinating. Would you not like to try *all* sorts of lives – one is so very small – but that is the satisfaction of writing – one can impersonate so many people –

Au revoir – dear friend.
Will you give my love to Cousin Ellie & Marjory?
I send you a great deal.

Your friend
K

75 Tinakori Rd
8 January, 1907

My dearest Sylvia –
I have to thank you for really charming letters – Please believe that I appreciate your letters really more than I can say – And your life sounds so desirable – also you gave me a sudden illuminating glimpse of chrysanthemums at that moment you might have been RLS. The New Year has come – I cannot really allow myself to think of it yet. I feel absolutely *ill* with grief and sadness – here – it is a nightmare – I feel that sooner or later I must wake up – & find myself in the heart of it all again – and look back upon the past months as . . . cobwebs – a hideous dream. Life here's impossible – I can't see how it can drag on – I have not one friend – and no prospect of one. My dear – I know nobody – and nobody cares to know me – There is nothing on earth to do – nothing to see – and my heart keeps flying off – Oxford Circus – Westminster Bridge at the Whistler hour – London by hansom – my old room – the meetings of the Swans – and a corner in the Library. It haunts me all so much – and I feel it must come back soon – How people ever wish to live here I cannot think –

Dear – I can't write anything – Tonight I feel too utterly hopelessly full of *Heimweh* [*homesickness*]. If you knew how

I hunger for it all – and for my friends – this absence of companionship – this starvation – that is what it is – I had better stop – hadn't I – because I can think of nothing joyous. I have been living too – in the atmosphere of Death. My Grandmother died on New Year's Eve – my first experience of a personal loss – it horrified me – the whole thing – Death never seemed revolting before – This place – steals your Youth – that is just what it does – I feel years and years older and sadder.

But I shall come back because here I should die – Goodnight. It is almost frightening to say goodnight across such a waste of waters – but dear – please – think of me always – in silence – or when our letters speak as

Ever your loving friend
Kass

By the Sea
4 March, 1908

My dear Cousin

I am – you see at last writing you a letter – because I must tell you – here tonight Sylvia – that I love you – far more than I loved you in England – that I would like – such an immeasurable great deal – to open wide this door – and welcome you in to the fire – and to the raging sea which breaks & foams against the yard fence.

Summer is over with us – there are briar berries in a green jar on the table – and an autumn storm is raging – The sea has never seemed so high – so fierce – It dashes against the rocks with a sound like thunder. Last night I was lying in my bunk. I could not sleep – I was thinking of you. Do you realise – I wonder – Cousin – how your voice charmed me at the Swanick meetings. I cannot exactly define what I mean – but it always made me feel I was very near you indeed – When I slept I dreamed that I came back to visit College – the only girl I knew in the Library was Marjory – she was not at all surprised to see me – I see her now – pushing back the ribbon in her hair – you know the way she had – and I asked for you – She said you were with Tudge – and then I saw you standing by the window in the Waiting room – My dear – I felt I must run and put my arms round you and just say '*Sylvia*' but you nodded & then walked away – and I did not move –

It was a terrible dream.

How much has happened since we two walked together to the New Barnet Station. My life has been so strange – full of either *sorrow* – or excitement – or disgust or happiness. In a year to have lived so much! And I have not made a friend. It is no good I can have men friends – they persist in asking for something else. Do you know Sylvia *five* men have asked me to marry them. And now you will put down this letter and say 'Kass is a second Sylvia Gifford', but it is the stupid truth – I have been reading – French & English – writing and lately have seen a great many Balls – and loved them – and dinners and receptions. They have such a different meaning for me now – and here. I have finished My First Book. If it never gets published – you shall laugh with me over its absurdities. Also I hope to leave for London next month – It is not unwise of me – it is the only thing to be done. I cannot live with Father – and I must get back because I know I shall be successful – look at the splendid tragic optimism of youth! One day – you must please know my brother. He knows you very well indeed – and he and I mean to live together – later on. I have never dreamed of loving a child as I love this boy. Do not laugh at me when I tell you I feel so maternal towards him. He is intensely affectionate and sensitive – he reads a great deal – draws with the most delicate sympathetic touch – and yet is a thoroughly brave healthy boy. Do not let me write of him – he is away at school – and if I go back next month we may not meet for years –

I hear, constantly, from Ida. You know I love her very much indeed – I am – Sylvia – the most completely unsatisfactory disappointing – *dull* friend it is possible to conceive – and when we meet again you will think – that is enough – *cela suffit* – Chaddie & I – with our maid – are living alone at this little cottage built on the rocks. It has only three rooms – two bedrooms fitted with bunks—and a wide living room – We had both been feeling wretchedly ill – and bored with Wellington – oh, the tedium vitae of 19 years! so have come here – where we bathe and row and walk in the bush or by the sea – and read – and I write – while she pursues the gentle art of fashioning camisoles. One could not be lonesome here – I seem to love it more each day – and the sea is a continually new sensation with me. Our life is absolutely free – absolutely happy – Oh, do come – my Friend & spend a week with me – Have you received one tenth of my wireless messages? I do not feel that I have been away from you one day. Now I can feel your hand clasping mine – but the *wasted* years when we might have been friends. But I was always afraid then – & I am now – that you do not know me – & when you do – you will hate me.

Still – Sylvia – I love you – very dearly – and I shall do so always.

Kass

# Family

*Much of the time family is the 'uninteresting' backdrop to our lives and it rarely gets much of a mention in the heartfelt pages of diaries and letters — except perhaps when we want to complain! The writers in this next section, however, have written about their families in a very distinct and unusual way . . .*

*Judy Allen and her mother had lived in her grandparents' house on Nettlecombe Avenue for much of her life. After her grandfather (Bup) died, Nettlecombe Avenue was sold, and her grandmother (Gagan) came to live with Judy and her mother elsewhere. Finally, Judy felt it was safe to write down her fears about the house. A turn-of-the-century detached house with garden might seem homely to some — to Judy, however, it was something else . . .*

## Judy Allen, aged 17

Sunday 27 July, 1958

I remember going home to Nettlecombe in the summer when the sun was mellow on the house and wheeling my bike in at the back gate, brushing past the beautiful hydrangeas, and smelling the roses, and when I see it like that, forgetting the monster inside, which Gagan never knew anyway, I can see why she must have been sad to leave it. But I knew — oh, it *does* sound silly — that it was an evil house and I *love* this home so much more than I ever did that one. And this one is *good*. Mummy felt the *feel* in Nettlecombe too, but she said it was just a bit disgruntled and unwelcoming. But I remember the footsteps crossing the big bedroom, the sound of the chair creaking, and then slow breathing as if something had come to watch over me all night, and not to protect me, but to give me frightening nightmares about the house itself. They never explained away the breathing. It wasn't the wind, or the curtains rustling, or the gas, or the cistern. It wasn't birds in the roof, or floorboards creaking, or my own breathing. That's why I say that house was evil. Every dream I ever had connected with the house was a nightmare.

I remember dreaming that I was in my bed and heard endless footsteps approaching and then a grinning face looked at me. I remember playing, or dreaming I played. hide and seek with a goblin, in the top room, and I remember the goblin hiding and waiting to pounce on me and my terrible fear ... I remember the night I heard Bup coming up the stairs and going to his dressing room and I called to him, to say goodnight, and he didn't answer. And I remember next morning telling him off about it and being told he hadn't come up ...

I remember the man in the homburg hat that I and one of my friends saw on the landing who wasn't there. And it wasn't a shadow either. We moved things to try and make a shadow of it, but we couldn't ... I remember the 'thing' in the boxroom, and above all I remember the awful terror, which was the greatest fear I have ever known, in the spare room when I slept there one night, and that was no shadow, nor wind, because I saw and heard nothing.

*During 1986 Charlotte Cooper's mother, Rosemary, had been suffering from unusual 'backaches'. In October of that year, on her eighteenth birthday, Charlotte found out that her mother had cancer. Rosemary started courses of chemotherapy and radio-therapy, but by January 1987 her health was deteriorating. With no one else to talk to who would really understand or who wouldn't get upset, Charlotte recorded in her diary her feelings throughout this difficult time.*

## Charlotte Cooper, aged 18

4 January, 1987

Mum has been in more and more pain these past few days. What can you do? She's eating more, which is good, but what can you do? You walk into her bedroom and she's moaning and sobbing like a child. There is nothing you can do to alleviate the pain for her. Later you ask if she's okay, and she always says she is, even when you know she's hurting all over. It makes me sick. I wish she'd tell us when she's hurting instead of moaning. And then she gets all silly and self-righteous as though she can bear it all herself. She needs help, but she's too proud to ask for it. I hate that.

6 January

I got home today at about 5.30. There was no one in. I at least hoped that I'd have someone to talk to. Mum has gone into hospital. I noticed the clock from the top of the TV had gone. When things like that happen I always think the worst. I think she's been rushed to hospital in a coma or something and any second now Dad or Paul will phone me and tell me that 'she died earlier in the afternoon'. I know it's stupid of me, but I remember what I said about Grandpa, 'You know he's going to die soon but whether "soon" is tomorrow or next year . . .'. That's when it hits you. I'm feeling quite depressed, but I want to wallow in it for the time being.

8 January

Mum is coming home on Saturday. I'm dreading seeing her. I can't see her during the week because of all the college stuff I have to do. I have learnt that you can never do enough work! Going back to Mum, Dad says she's on morphine and it's doing her the world of good. They don't say that about smackheads, do they? He said they've taken the addictive ingredient out of it, but I don't believe any doctors any more. I'm scared.

10 January

What I saw of Mum today depressed me so much. After all these reports about how chirpy and happy she was, and then I go and see her.

I wanted to cry but I didn't and couldn't. It was like Alex in *A Clockwork Orange* where he's forced to watch the horror on the screens. I felt like someone was holding my neck and making me watch what was going on. At least when she's in the other room I don't have to watch. She was writhing in pain and all I could do was sit and watch. I felt like I was rooted to the spot.

My mum is hardly recognisable. She has got so thin and fragile. On the inside of her right elbow and left wrist she has horrific-looking bruises where blood has been taken and she has not healed properly. I am waiting for her hair to go.

I put myself in her place all the time. At least me and Paul and Jeremy and Dad have other lives at work and college to go back to. Mum can't lock her illness away for the weekend whilst she has fun. She won't be home for a little while yet. I feel f***ing lonely tonight. Lonely and guilty.

## 15 January

I feel so selfish and guilty. I feel like I'm using Mum's illness to get sympathy from everyone.

I can't imagine what it's going to be like without her. No one has said that she's going to die but my mind always goes into overdrive when I'm being kept in the dark about something. I keep hoping that, sometime in the future, I can look back on this period of my life and laugh at myself for being so silly and blowing things out of proportion. At the moment though I can't see anything like that ever happening. I can only think of how much I am going to miss my mum.

## 18 January

Mum isn't too bad today. I always thought that I would be level-headed in situations like these, but I'm not! I tend to panic inside, and jump to terrible conclusions. After all is said and done I am glad that she is at home. Even though she's heavily sedated all the time, I know how well/ill she is by watching her and talking to her, not from Dad's reports.

## 20 January

Speaking to Mum this afternoon took a weight off my shoulders. It's hard to tell whether it's her talking or the morphine. I'm still tempted to try some. Maybe, maybe not. She said that I seem to be immersing myself in my work and that I ought not to push myself too far. Ha! She knows. There's no way I could cope without work.

## 27 January

Last night Paul came into my room. He told me that two

weeks ago Dad had gone to find the truth from Mum's doctor. The doctor said that Mum hasn't got any chance; she has cancer in so many parts of her that she is almost certainly going to die soon.

This is true. It's all my worst fears.

I cried a lot and felt stupid and puny and terrible.

I went to college today through a need to get out. I cried a bit but it was only self-indulgent; I was crying out of self-pity, not because of what is happening to Mum.

I am very tired. I wish I could go to sleep for ten years.

I didn't see Jenny today, I really missed her. Fran was really nice.

It's time for Mum's pills now. I'll go round the shops in a minute, then I'll prepare dinner and do some homework.


30 January

I didn't go into college today because there would have been no one to look after Mum. Jenny came round whilst I was doing the housework. I think her and Paul are going to get together. I don't want to be left alone again.

I have been having vivid dreams about Mum. I'm sleeping so much. I wish I could just dream my life away. I feel as though I'm being taken apart piece by piece and it HURTS.


3 February

Mum had a bad day. No one was with her until I got home at around three. Because she is so out of it on morphine she couldn't remember the times to take her pills. Dad keeps saying things like 'We'll get her on the exercise bike', or 'She can go round and do the shopping', crap like that, for his benefit I suppose. She wanted to hoover and polish her room, and clean the toilet, make dinner. She managed about ten minutes of polishing before getting exhausted. I rubbed her back and helped her along. I wish we'd all stop lying to each other and face the truth together.

26 February
College today was all right. At last we are moving forward with our group piece.

I wore a pair of Steve's Converse boots today. It was nice I could feel the shape of his foot on the sole of the boot.

27 February
I had my early morning rehearsal, which was good because I got to use all the lights and blocks and stuff. I was really nervous in front of everyone. After a couple of run-throughs I felt okay. They clapped at the end and I felt shy.

After rehearsals this evening we went to the pub and Karin bought us all drinks on the pretext that she is now earning. Steve drove me home. First we went to the John Lyon and I had a glass of cider. I saw Lee Birch down there. He really brought back memories of when we all used to go to those Harrow Leisure Under 18s discos. I used to really fancy him and wish and wish and wish.

Anyway . . . Steve came round to my house and we sat and talked. Dad and Paul were very pissed. As usual I suppose. Then Paul came up and monopolised the conversation. Sometimes I really hate him. He just went on and on and really patronised us. Steve was really lovely, and he left at about 2.30. Paul said cruel things to me: 'Do you remember that rhyme "The clock struck and the old man died"?' Mum is dying; he plays on that and frightens me. I went to bed.

Mum is back in hospital.

## 1 March

Dad went to see Mum today. Apparently she's much better. Her mind is back in the 'right' place because of a drip they put her on. I hate the whole medical profession.

Today has been unremarkable. I got up late, did the ironing, wrote some letters, etc., etc., you know the score.

This week is going to be very busy. I'm really looking forward to seeing Alan on Friday, but nervous too in case something dreadful happens to Mum while I'm gone. Last night I was sure Mum was going to die this week, now I'm not so sure, but I was very frightened yesterday.

It's hard to gather up my thoughts. This evening I shared a bottle of wine with Dad and I feel quite tipsy. It's making writing my diary harder than ever.

## 2 March

Today has been a strain. Everybody was at everybody else's throats in Drama. I spent the evening alone. Jayne County phoned to say that the Hippodrome thing has been put back a week. Just as well, really. I got a costume for it – it's hideous.

Dad came home from hospital today to say that he'll be surprised if Mum makes it through the night. Apparently today she had a heart attack.

I'm scared. Really frightened. I can't even think of much to write. Suddenly it's becoming real. I keep thinking about little things, like dismantling her bed, and seeing her pictures that she painted, and books that she read. How am I going to handle that? I don't know what it's going to do to Dad. Even the funeral. All I can think about is death. What's going to happen?

3 March
There's not much to say. She's not dead yet but she will be soon.

We have all been at the hospital. Mum is unrecognisable.

4 March
See yesterday.

5 March
My Mum died this morning at 12.45 am. Dad said she was 'considerate until the end' and died just as *Sportsnight* was finishing. I love her.

8 March
I haven't been able to write anything these past couple of days. I'm too depressed to do anything. Too depressed to write even! That's saying something. I've been ill too.

F***.

If only things didn't look so bleak. I wish I could get out and start again on my own. What's going to happen? I never thought I'd catch myself feeling, and thinking, and wanting to die.

The funeral is on Wednesday.

## 9 March

I dreamt it was Mum's birthday last night. I sorted out all her make-up and stuff today, and jewellery. I was crying a lot. There was a letter amongst all her bits and pieces from someone only Mum had ever heard of, saying things like 'We prayed for you last night.' If I met her I'd kick her teeth in. 'She is with the Lord now.' F*** HER.

Dad is downstairs playing that Adagio music. I know how he feels.

I went round the shops and I had to tell people at the bank that Mum had died. I had to tell the woman from up the road and the butcher. It's so pathetic.

## 10 March

Jenny came round today and I enjoyed her company. It's the funeral tomorrow. Jayne phoned and said how sorry she was. Well. I'll be brave. I got a letter from Marion which annoyed me, maybe I'll write to her, maybe I'll not. There's not much to say. I'm tired. I can't wait until it's all over.

*This entry from Anne Frank's diary was written on her fifteenth birthday, and she reflects on many of the things she had written about over the past two years in hiding. Anne always wanted to be a writer and, although her life was cruelly cut short, her lively and honest diary became a classic in itself.*

*Living in close quarters, and united by their fears of discovery, the group of people in the Secret Annexe became very intimate – like a large, extended family. Being the youngest person there, Anne found that she was frequently criticised, told off and generally accused of bad behaviour! However, she found solace in*

*her affection for her friend Peter van Daan, and in allowing*
*herself to have hopes, and sometimes plans, for the future.*

## Anne Frank, aged 15

Tuesday 13 June, 1944
*Dearest Kit,*

Another birthday has gone by, so I'm now fifteen. I received quite a few gifts: Springer's five-volume art history book, a set of underwear, two belts, a handkerchief, two pots of yoghurt, a pot of jam, two honey biscuits (small), a botany book from Father and Mother, a gold bracelet from Margot, a sticker album from the Van Daans, Biomalt and sweet peas from Dussel, sweets from Miep, sweets and exercise-books from Bep, and the high point: the book *Maria Theresa* and three slices of full-cream cheese from Mr Kugler. Peter gave me a lovely bouquet of peonies; the poor boy had put a lot of effort into finding a present, but nothing quite worked out.

The invasion is still going splendidly, in spite of the miserable weather – pouring rains, strong winds and high seas . . . From our position here in Fort Annexe, it's difficult to gauge the mood of the Dutch. No doubt many people are glad the idle (!) British have finally rolled up their sleeves and got down to work. Those who keep claiming they don't want to be occupied by the British don't realise how unfair they're being. Their line of reasoning boils down to this: Britain must fight, struggle and sacrifice its sons to liberate Holland and the other occupied countries. After that the British shouldn't remain in Holland: they should offer their most abject apologies to all the occupied countries, restore the Dutch East Indies to its rightful owner and then return, weakened and impoverished, to Britain. What a bunch of idiots. And yet, as I've already said, many Dutch people can be counted among their ranks. What would have become of Holland and its neighbours if Britain had signed a peace treaty with Germany, as it's had ample opportunity to do? Holland would have become German, and that would have been the end of that!

All those Dutch people who still look down on the British, scoff at Britain and its government of ageing lords, call them cowards, yet hate the Germans, should be given a good shaking, the way you'd plump up a pillow. Maybe that would straighten out their jumbled brains!

Wishes, thoughts, accusations and reproaches are swirling around in my head. I'm not really as conceited as many people think; I know my various faults and shortcomings better than anyone else, but there's one difference: I also know that I want to change, will change and already have changed greatly!

Why is it, I often ask myself, that everyone still thinks I'm so pushy and such a know-it-all? Am I really so arrogant? Am *I* the one who's so arrogant, or are they? It sounds silly, I know, but I'm not going to cross out that last sentence, because it's not as silly as it seems. Mrs van Daan and Dussel, my two chief accusers, are known to be totally unintelligent and, not to put too fine a point on it, just plain 'stupid'! Stupid people usually can't bear it when others do something better than they do; the best examples of this are those two dunces, Mrs van Daan and Dussel. Mrs van D. thinks I'm stupid because I don't suffer so much from this ailment as she does, she thinks I'm pushy because she's even pushier, she thinks my dresses are too short because hers are even shorter, and she thinks I'm such a know-it-all because she talks twice as much as I do about topics she knows nothing about. The same goes for Dussel. But one of my favourite sayings is 'Where there's smoke there's fire', and I readily admit I'm a know-it-all.

What's so difficult about my personality is that I scold and curse myself much more than anyone else does; if Mother adds her advice, the pile of sermons becomes so thick that I despair of ever getting through them. Then I talk back and start contradicting everyone until the old familiar Anne refrain inevitably crops up again: 'No one understands me!'

This phrase is part of me, and as unlikely as it may seem, there's a kernel of truth in it. Sometimes I'm so deeply buried under self-reproaches that I long for a word of comfort to help me dig myself out again. If only I had someone who took my feelings seriously. Alas, I haven't yet found that person, so the search must go on.

I know you're wondering about Peter, aren't you, Kit? It's true, Peter loves me, not as a girlfriend, but as a friend. His affection grows day by day, but some mysterious force is holding us back, and I don't know what it is.

Sometimes I think my terrible longing for him was over-exaggerated. But that's not true, because if I'm unable to go to his room for a day or two, I long for him as desperately as I ever did. Peter is kind and good, and yet I can't deny that he's disappointed me in many ways. I especially don't care for his dislike of religion, his talk of food and various things of that nature. Still, I'm firmly convinced that we'll stick to our agreement never to quarrel. Peter is peace-loving, tolerant and extremely easygoing. He lets me say a lot of things to him that he'd never accept from his mother. He's making a determined effort to remove the blots from his copybook and keep his affairs in order. Yet why does he hide his innermost self and never allow me access? Of course, he's much more closed than I am, but I know from experience (even though I'm constantly being accused of knowing all there is to know in theory, but not in practice) that in time, even the most uncommunicative types will long as much, or even more, for someone to confide in.

Peter and I have both spent our contemplative years in the Annexe. We often discuss the future, the past and the present, but as I've already told you, I miss the real thing, and yet I know it exists!

Is it because I haven't been outdoors for so long that I've become so mad about nature? I remember a time when a magnificent blue sky, chirping birds, moonlight and budding blossoms wouldn't have captivated me. Things have changed since I came here. One night during Whitsun, for instance, when it was so hot, I struggled to keep my eyes open until eleven-thirty so I could get a good look at the moon, all on my own for once. Alas, my sacrifice was in vain, since there was too much glare and I couldn't risk opening a window. Another time, several months ago, I happened to be upstairs one night when the window was open. I didn't go back down until it had to be closed again. The dark, rainy evening, the wind, the racing clouds, had me spellbound; it was the first time in a year and a half that I'd seen the night face-to-face. After that evening my longing to see it again was even greater than my fear of burglars, a dark rat-infested house or police raids. I went downstairs all by myself and looked out of the windows in the kitchen and private office. Many people think nature is beautiful, many people sleep from time to time under the starry sky, and many people in hospitals and prisons long for the day when they'll be free to enjoy what nature has to offer. But few are as isolated and cut off as we are from the joys of nature, which can be shared by rich and poor alike.

It's not just my imagination – looking at the sky, the clouds, the moon and the stars really does make me feel calm and hopeful. It's much better medicine than valerian or bromide. Nature makes me feel humble and ready to face every blow with courage!

As luck would have it, I'm only able – except for a few rare occasions – to view nature through dusty curtains tacked over dirt-caked windows; it takes the pleasure out of looking. Nature is the one thing for which there is no substitute!

One of the many questions that have often bothered me is why women have been, and still are, thought to be so inferior to men. It's easy to say it's unfair, but that's not enough for me; I'd really like to know the reason for this great injustice!

Men presumably dominated women from the very beginning because of their greater physical strength; it's men who earn a living, beget children and do as they please . . . Until recently, women silently went along with this, which was stupid, since the longer it's kept up, the more deeply entrenched it becomes. Fortunately, education, work and progress have opened women's eyes. In many countries they've been granted equal rights; many people, mainly women, but also men, now realise how wrong it was to tolerate this state of affairs for so long. Modern women want the right to be completely independent!

But that's not all. Women should be respected as well! Generally speaking, men are held in great esteem in all parts of the world, so why shouldn't women have their share? Soldiers and war heroes are honoured and commemorated, explorers are granted immortal fame, martyrs are revered, but how many people look upon women too as soldiers?

In the book *Men against Death* I was greatly struck by the fact that in childbirth alone, women commonly suffer more pain, illness and misery than any war hero ever does. And what's her reward for enduring all that pain? She gets pushed aside when she's disfigured by birth, her children soon leave, her beauty is gone. Women, who struggle and suffer pain to ensure the continuation of the human race, make much tougher and more courageous soldiers than all those big-mouthed freedom-fighting heroes put together!

I don't mean to imply that women should stop having children; on the contrary, nature intended them to, and that's the way it should be. What I condemn are our system of values and the men who don't acknowledge how great, difficult, but ultimately beautiful women's share in society is.

I agree completely with Paul de Kruif, the author of this book, when he says that men must learn that birth is no longer thought of as inevitable and unavoidable in those parts of the world we consider civilised. It's easy for men to talk – they don't and never will have to bear the woes that women do!

I believe that in the course of the next century the notion that it's a woman's duty to have children will change and make way for the respect and admiration of all women, who bear their burdens without complaint or a lot of pompous words!

Yours, Anne M Frank

# Relationships

*Relationships appear again and again in diaries and letters. To whom else, but your trusted diary or best friend, can you confide the highs and lows experienced with your heart's desire?*

*Eileen Fairweather, over several years in her diary, recorded her love for French boys — which began with a trip to Switzerland at the age of thirteen and culminated in her disastrous relationship with Alain two years later! (These experiences were to provide the background material for her novels* French Letters *and* French Leave.*) In the meantime she started a Saturday job to find the money for more trips abroad, worried about her parents and sister, and kept (English) admirers Charlie and Jimmy interested, but in their place!*

## Eileen Fairweather, aged 13–15

Sunday 31 December, 1967
The happiest day of my Swiss school hol! First time abroad fab. Mass, lunch at FRENCH BOYS' CHALET. They asked us to stay and dance. Great French bloke called Richard — the first time I've danced close with a boy!

Monday 1 January, 1968
Party at hotel, danced *close* all night with Luch, Catu's brother. Fab Good Night Kiss — first boy ever! I was pretty popular with boys in my sexy red dress.

Tuesday 2 January
Luch has dropped me! I hate him for it, cos he's shy, and to dance, hold hands and kiss me was, for a shy bloke, something! Richard is mad on me. Let him kiss me — but Luch has won my heart!

Wednesday 3 January
Party at hotel after great day skiing. Frenchies are gone –
au revoir! Luch hardly danced with me at all. A guy called
Roberto is mad on me, but I want Luch – he wanted me
at New Year, why not now?

Friday 5 January
Caught train. Goodbye Switzerland! I leant out of the
train and wept my heart out for the beauty and sadness.
Of leaving – my first kisses – not knowing why Luch
dumped me.
    What a fab holiday!

Sunday 7 January
I'm going to get a Saturday job to earn money to go to
Switzerland next year. Told Mum all about Luch – she
was great, dead sympathetic.
    I learnt a hell of a lot on that holiday – boys, skiing and
God (prayed a lot) – I'm grateful.

Wednesday 17 January
Job hunting – no luck yet. Guess what – through Jo in
the other class and her Frog boyfriend, Richard has asked
me to write to him. Oh hunk of flesh, I will!

Saturday 27 January
STARTED AT NI TONY'S, *the hairdresser's* as a Saturday
girl! I feel so lovely, and kind of responsible, with a little
job, earning £1 a week – I'm going to Switzerland again
next year! Hard work but worth it!

Wednesday 28 February
Went in to Tony's for a couple of hours after school. Poor old Mum is run down by everything – especially Dad (as usual).

Saturday 2 March
Got eight shillings for shampooing today! Great. I get on quite well with the customers. Nice day but tired. Richard writes super letters now.

Sunday 3 March
Went to Doloures' – did some gardening, had tea, 6.30 Mass. Enjoyed it v. much because *done with friends.*

Came home and Dad – I've been ignoring him and sticking up for Mum – gave me a quiet 'chat'. My God, he upset me!

I love my mother so much, but somehow he has 'cooled' my feelings towards her. I now know she is very ill. How I wish she would let the doctor help her. Dad says she should be in a mental hospital – or is she just unhappy because Dad's always shouting?

Monday 4 March
I was so upset at school and tired from lack of sleep – I was worrying about poor Mum – I could not concentrate. Where will it all end?

Sunday 24 March
Mother's Day. Gave Mum a box of Milk Tray and my love! Today all rotten with Anne. She will be 16 in one month, yet she has left home. So, she can't stand the rows any more. I'm not even letting Doloures know about Anne going.

**Sunday 14 April**
Easter Sunday. Really lovely day. Anne came. Easter eggs for all! We got on well – !!!

**Saturday 20 April**
'Ugh' day at work. Didn't feel – or act – very well! Got seven and a half shillings tips and told Helen she was getting big-headed.

**Wednesday 24 April**
Saw Anne briefly and gave her ten shillings for a birthday present. I miss her! Never would have thought it poss, but I do!

**Saturday 6 May**
New girl at work. She's only a Saturday girl like me – Pam – I detest her. She nicked all my shampoo ladies and doesn't have *my* standards.

**Friday 8 June**
Went to Marion O'G's party. It was yuck! No boys turned up and did she lose face! Oh well!

**Friday 2 August**
Last night went to another party that never was. Fabulous French bloke called Michel! But no party!

Went shopping to Wood Green, bought black mini skirt, lime-green crêpe shirt, blue cardigan – total cost, six pounds and ten shillings!

**Saturday 24 August**
Work. About 8.30 pm Charlie and Jimmy from

discussion group called. Went for a drive then parked and talked until 12 pm. They are great but thought *que moi j'aime les femmes* – that I am a lesbian – because I don't fancy them(!) but I told them otherwise and ended up having a fab chat!

Sunday 25 August
Slept late. Discussion group. Jimmy had no petrol so Charlie walked me home – hasn't changed his ideas . . .

Monday 26 August
Charlie went on holiday to Wales. Jimmy wanted me to play tennis with him, but I pottered around house on my own instead.

Thursday 29 August
Received a lovely letter from Charlie in Wales and a card from his brother who has, I think, a bit of a crush on me too!

Sunday 1 September
Jimmy took me to see *Decline and Fall*, from the novel by Evelyn Waugh. Went to a café after and had great chat about books and so on. Walked through Trafalgar Square. I defined our relationship as platonic. He's so nice, but I just don't fancy him. He very amiably accepted this – however, he cannot have enjoyed it, as his later poems show . . .

Wednesday 4 September
Charlie back from Wales. Went round to Jimmy's.

Monday 9 September
Charlie and Jimmy came round, asked me to go to

Charlie's school to get his exam results. School tomorrow so said no.

Tuesday 10 September
I asked Charlie to take me somewhere decent, but I called off the date he made to take me to see *Camelot*, as I'd lots of homework.

Saturday 14 September
Jimmy took me to see *Wait Until Dark*. Told me he'd written me the poem I received yesterday, 'Fill for me a brimming bowl'.

He's really gentle, Jimmy — considerate, kind and an interesting companion, but I just cannot think of either him or Charlie as boyfriends. Neither will ever understand this, I think.

Went to Wimpy afterwards.

Tuesday 17 September
Charlie and Jimmy kept calling round. I pretended to be out, but was eventually in. Jimmy plucked up the courage to give me 'a wee sonnet', another love poem!

Sunday 22 September
Jimmy took me to discussion group. Charlie v. v. rude to me — ignored me, then flirted with everyone else. Said goodbye and wished him good luck for school (he's expecting to get expelled). Felt a fool.

Sunday 29 September
Jimmy was going to take me out, but I couldn't be bothered so phoned and said I had a headache.

Tuesday 1 October
Went round to Jimmy's after school. He gave me some novels: Evelyn Waugh, John Steinbeck, Hemingway. Not really my kind of authors but I was glad to have something from my dear Jimmy. He took me home and I pecked him on the cheek by way of saying goodbye: tomorrow he's off to university.

Saturday 28 June, 1969
It was Marie-Therese's 21st today. Mum held a party for her, seeing as she's the niece of her friend Sister Jean Vianney and away from home. Marie-Therese invited four boys from France. Charlie went up London airport to help us look for them as we weren't sure if they had got Marie-Therese's letter which changed arrangements. I didn't think it was necessary to ask Charlie this favour, but Anne panicked and persuaded me to: I feel really awful to have used him.

2 am: French boys arrived. Even though middle of the night they wanted to go uptown, to *Soho*!!! Anne took them, I refused.

Midday, after the Catechism class I teach, we took them to the place Marie-Therese works. Doloures came, very shy. Got back late, prepared for party. About 80 people must have come in all! 7.30–3 am. One of the French boys, Alain, danced a lot with me.

There was nearly some trouble with some anti-French people but all in all party fabulous, really enjoyed it. Wore my new white dress, with white tights and white rose in my hair – given me by Sandra when she arrived. It was a lovely gesture.

## Sunday 29 June

Cleared up. Marie-Therese came at 10 pm, having seen boys off at air terminal. Told me Alain found me intelligent, nice, attractive, etc.! He wants to write to me! V. excited because at first I disliked him, but well . . . rather fancied him in a way I suppose!

## Friday 19 December

Broke up from school – rushed to Heathrow to meet Alain from Paris! Took all the letters he's written me since July for good luck. Great, great chat coming back! But Alain doesn't understand why Mum and Dad won't let him stay (v. strict). Marie-Therese has got him digs.

## Saturday 20 December

Small party at Marie-Therese's. Draggy.

## Sunday 21 December

Took Alain round Victoria, etc. Mass at Westminster Cathedral, National Gallery. Not going well. Alain wants to go to pubs, but I'm not old enough. He asked me to suggest a 'nice restaurant' and I took him to Wimpy. He hated it and was v.rude about the English putting vinegar on chips.

## Monday 22 December

Went to see the City with Alain, then Tower of London, then shopping and Foyles. Home about 8.30.

## Tuesday 23 December

Went with Alain to Madame Tussaud's, Planetarium, etc.

He was very bored and showed it. We went to Marie-Therese's and had a drink with her.

HORRIBLE.

Wednesday 24 December
Went shopping, Anne, Marie-Therese, Alain and me.

Poor Mummy had had a row with Dad when we got home.

Thursday 25 December
Midnight Mass – nice. Sat up till 5 am. Alain gave me a novel and a Christian Dior scarf (!). Got up late. Just ate, watched TV – really dull.

Poor Anne v. v. miserable about her ex-boyfriend – she was meant to be with him and his family this Christmas.

And Alain sulked about the 'boring' way we cooked our chicken.

Friday 26 December
Went to v. modern BEA terminal to see Alain off at 4 pm. Long, long wait. It was *horrible* sitting there, waiting for him to go. Didn't talk much.

So disappointed. Alain had kept hinting in his letters he wanted to marry me, seemed so romantic. Now I know he's just a Frog snob! I think I might have a *broken heart*.

Saw a gorgeous French boy at the terminal. What a shame Frogs are so hunky!

*Relationships don't always start off well, especially when it's your first boyfriend. Millie Murray confided the traumatic start to her relationship with 'D' in her diary. Unlikely as it seems, she and 'D' were together for ten years — and when it ended Millie was so relieved she stayed single for another ten! Perhaps she should have learnt something from the inauspicious start — but then again, she did have some fun along the way . . .*

## Millie Murray, aged 15

Friday 14 June, 1974

School dragged today. I think it was the hot weather and the thought that for the first time ever my mum was letting me go out with my sisters. Debbie, being the eldest, didn't think it was a problem, but Marcia was complaining. Said she wasn't allowed out at 15, why should I be? Thank goodness my mum wasn't listening to her — she was more concerned about us coming back at the right time.

All day long I have been daydreaming about what it's going to be like. Marcia is letting me wear her old smock dress with matching hot pants and Debbie is letting me wear her old platforms from Chelsea Cobblers! I think the reason they have lent me their clothes is because they don't want me to show them up by wearing my out-of-date ones.

I don't care what the reason is, just as long as I'm looking fit and trendy!

Sunday 16 June — 6 pm

Phew! What a weekend! I don't think I'm ever going to be the same person again. My life has changed. Sounds a bit dramatic even to me as I write this, but it's amazing that in a couple of days, life as I know it has disappeared and something else has taken its place.

Six of us went out to the football dance, held in Forest Gate at the Eagle and Child pub. Marcia stopped moaning after a while and by the time we set off, I was really excited. It was packed out with people and for the first hour all I was worried about was that I had enough hairpins holding down my false afro puffs. I kept having terrible thoughts that one would drop off, and the whole world (well, the pub) would see the real state of my hair. Shame! Thank goodness nothing bad like that did happen and I was just beginning to let myself get into the groove of the reggae beat, when someone called my name. I couldn't believe it – it was Kim and Janet from school, looking stylish and cool. After we had shouted at each other – 'What you doing here?', 'How long you been here?', 'Who are you with?' – we started to get into the swing of things.

That's when I met him.

He reckoned he had been watching me all night and was waiting for the right time to come over and talk to me.

I was so nervous I felt sick, Kim answered his questions for me because my tongue was stuck to the roof of my mouth and I couldn't talk. He asked if I wanted a drink and Kim said, 'Three cherry B's'.

He went and got them.

The thing is while we were in a three-way conversation (even though I didn't say a word), I was giving him the once over and I wasn't too happy with what I saw. I know that being 15 you're not supposed to be too mature and know what's what. But I'm not stupid and I know what's real and what's fantasy. Looking at him, I thought, I'll just drink his Cherry B and go back to fantasy!

The dance finished at 10.30 and by the time I got outside it was coming up to eleven and I couldn't find my sisters.

D (code name) said that he knew my sister Marcia and if I just stood by the hot dog stand outside he would find her for me. I was glad at that stage that Kim and Janet were with me even though I was having to push down the panic that was trying hard to burst out of my mouth.

D came back at 11.35 – no sisters – he reckoned he couldn't find them. The panic gushed out and Kim and Janet had to hold on to me. I was terrified of being out at nearly midnight on my own. All that time waiting for him to find my sisters and I could have got a bus home.

He walked off. I was crying by now and Kim was telling me to stop being a baby. She didn't understand.

D came back and said that his friend was going to give us a lift in his car. A huge load fell off my back. I jumped into the car with Kim, Janet and D and it wasn't till the car stopped that I realised that it wasn't outside my house.

I started crying again.

D tried to put his arm around me to console me, and was telling me rubbish about how, if I came inside, he would call a cab. Kim and Janet and D's mate rushed into the house. (Which, when I gave it a sneaky peep, was very large, and the thought that D must have some money did flick through my mind.) But, fear was gripping me.

All the things my mum told me concerning boys and babies came into my mind and wouldn't go. What made it worse was that Kim and Janet kept coming to the window and telling me to come in. I wouldn't. The other thing that was on my mind was that I didn't know what shift my dad was on, and my mum had only let me go on condition that I stuck with my sisters and came home

with them — it was unthi...
getting home after my dad,...
bolts the door.

I didn't want to do it but it...
some game, so what else could...
of my voice! He moved fast. N...
but he gave me £2.50 and his t...

I left Kim and Janet there.

My mum was up when I got i... ...was worried sick about me and before I could explain she started firing licks with her big hands across my head. My two sisters were in the kitchen drinking Milo. They laughed at me and said that they'd told Kim to tell me to go home. I started crying again, but this time it was more because I was relieved to be home in one piece. At least D hadn't been lying. When we heard the key in the lock I knew that my dad was home, and I ran upstairs to the safety of my bedroom.

Thursday 20 June — 11 pm
What a day. I had told Sandra and Carol all about the football dance and D. When I met up with Kim and Janet on Monday they said that I was a kid and I should try growing up and finding out all about real life.

Carol, loyal as ever, said that she had heard that they were a bit loose and I reckon that's true. Anyway, I don't care what they say about me.

At lunchtime today we went down the market. The fruit stall at the top end of the market was selling grapes really cheap so we decided that that was going to be our lunch. Halfway through the market we pretended that we were drunk and started acting like the winos down in were looking at us but we didn't care. the chip shop at the other end and a couple rom my class stopped me and said that someone looking for me, but I pretended that I couldn't understand what they were talking about. I wish I had listened.

Out of nowhere popped this tall bloke with a white motorcycle crash helmet on. I didn't know who he was at first, till he took the helmet off – then I felt I was going to pass out. He said 'Millie' and I didn't wait to hear any more. I ran. Back at school, Sandra and Carol said that I moved faster than electricity.

After school I didn't wait around just in case he turned up. All evening I felt ill wondering if he was going to turn up at my house.

He didn't.

Friday 21 June – 7 pm

D was waiting for me outside school. It was weird – instead of feeling frightened I felt stupid. He had his bike with him and the white helmet was hanging on the handle. He walked me to the flats at the end of my road and a terrible thing happened. My half slip, which used to be Debbie's and was therefore old and worn out, gave its last stretch and collapsed in a heap at my feet. Both D and I were shocked. I knew it was my slip but by the look on his face he must've thought it was my big blooming knickers! My heart flipped, and I wanted the ground to open up and swallow me. Nothing doing. I bent down and picked up the slip and stuffed it in my pocket. My knees were like jelly and I was getting psyched up for a run again, when D grabbed my arm. I didn't quite catch what he said, but he kissed me on the cheek and that was all I could bear – I took off again.

When I told Sharon on the phone what happened she roared with laughter and even I had to see the funny side of it. Thinking about D, I wonder if I should go out with him (every time he sees me he asks, and I keep saying no). I could just use him as an experiment – having never had a boyfriend before, I could practise on him. He is quite a nice boy really, well, man – he's 19!!!!!!

Saturday 22 June
I've just come back from the phone box. My hand was shaking like a leaf as I dialled D's number, and having Sharon next to me breathing down my ear made me feel worse. I told D I would be his girlfriend. He wanted to come and pick me up there and then on his motorbike – I asked him if he was mad? Mum and dad think I'm far too young to have boyfriends – especially not if they're 19 years old!

I told D to meet me down the market at 3.30 pm – and told my mum I was going to Sharon's house. She told me to be home for 7.30 at the latest, as my dad's shift finished at 8 and if I was still out when he got home she wouldn't be held responsible for his actions.

Sunday 23 June
When D turned up yesterday, Sharon took off, with promises that I'd phone her today. D had borrowed his dad's car and took me to Ilford. We sat in the Wimpy restaurant until 6.30. He drove me to the flats at the end of my road and while I was telling him about my family he kissed me. I didn't know what to expect and I still

can't put into words what I felt. The only thing I remember is that my heart was racing. When we (he) finished his eyes were sort of glazed. I felt a bit silly and looked down at my knees. When I looked up I got the shock of my life. My dad was coming towards the car. He must have taken a short cut through the flats. I didn't know whether to jump out the car or what.

I ducked.

I could hear D asking what was wrong. I squeaked 'Drive to my house.' D zoomed up the road, and I prayed that my dad wouldn't see me get out of the car.

Sitting in the front room I was holding my breath as my dad's key turned in the lock. But he just popped his head in the front room and then went upstairs.

What an escape. I wonder if D still wants me for a girlfriend?

*In Sarra Manning's heartfelt letter to a friend, she tells of a relationship that started badly and then went straight downhill. However, she never lost sight of what she wanted, and the relationship's short demise was due to her not settling for second best!*

## Sarra Manning, aged 18

Late night, Maudlin Street
February, 1989

Hello Angel

I'm finally coming out of the slough of despair – there would have been no point in writing to you when things were at their worst. Of course you knew that my future was completely unsettled – no permanent job or hint of higher education in sight – life could hardly have got worse, but it did. I'll tell you the whole sordid little tale. It started when I was in my second year at college and this boy started on one of the engineering courses, I'd seen him around and he looked rather like Jim Reid from the Jesus and Mary Chain so I labelled him Thin Jim. I quite fancied him and we exchanged curious looks, but you know how looks change into animosity. He started going out with a real Sharon and before our eyes she transformed herself into a female Thin Jim which provided us with plenty of scope for gossip. It got so bad in the end that to sort things out, I became incredibly brave and talked to her. I kept bumping into them at gigs and me and him developed a friendship of sorts. After college it petered out.

When I was back in London after dropping out of Coventry, I found out that he'd rung a couple of times, so I sent him a Crimbo card. The Thursday before Xmas Eve he rang up and asked me out for a drink as he was depressed because he'd split up with the Sharon. You get the picture so far?

So we met for a drink and he came on really strong and I just pretended to be terribly amused. I hang around with gay blokes the whole time so I held his hand like it was no big deal. But all he wanted to do was kiss me and I understandably thought that the bastard was using me. He waited with me at the bus–stop and all his jokes didn't detract away from his intentions, so I slapped him around the face which threw him a bit. He was a little piqued and wouldn't speak to me but when I got on the bus, he mouthed the words 'phone me'. I did.

On Xmas Eve after only two vodkas I got quite

inexplicably drunk. He got me drunker and drunker and one thing led to another and then he was snogging my face (and lipstick) off. Now, even through a haze of alcohol, I was kinda detached. I still thought I was being used and the kisses were as treacherous as ever, but what the hell – he was passable, lots of girls fancied him and he seemed to be interested in me. We frenched with abandon at the bus-stop, or rather he attacked my neck, my ears and my mouth with fervour while I kept lookout for the bus.

And then we were going out. We saw each other every night but I hated his kisses. He was so predictable. He'd kiss me four times on his lips and then shove his tongue down my throat. I let him go a certain way before putting up barriers, which he was surprising sympathetic about, but after only a couple of days, it all went wrong. He couldn't handle my sarcasm and poor little insecure thing that he was, he took it all too seriously. I knew in my heart of hearts, even if he didn't realise it, that he was using me and I couldn't grasp why certain things I said would upset him so much. He was jealous of Johnny (my best friend) and couldn't believe that our friendship was non-romantic. All his kissing and groping made me feel very vulnerable (you now have my heart on paper!). I wanted to see if I'd FEEL something but I never did.

So you have him with all his little prejudices and desires and me not knowing what the hell I was doing and not wanting to share myself with anybody as he constantly badgered me, 'What are you thinking? Why are you looking at me like that?'

It's New Year's Eve by now and I get a phone call from him. He'd just told the Sharon that we were going out and she was very upset and wanted to come down. I told him that he was on his own with this one and that he could come round to mine later with Johnny and we'd go out. When he finally puts in an appearance he's all sulky and won't tell me what's happened and just sits there and wants me to comfort him. I know his usual girlfriends would kiss it all better but I'm not 'woman' enough. Johnny turns up and the atmosphere becomes positively glacial. Johnny's Christmas present to me was a framed picture of himself and my totally not-suspicious boyfriend accuses us of having an illicit affair. I keep running downstairs and telling my parents that I don't want to go out at all.

Anyway, we begin our festivities in the pub. I hold his hand and try to cheer him up but I end up with a mood that's ten times worse than his. Now he's off-loaded his misery into me, he's chipper and I'm furious. I refuse to let him buy me a drink (which he later confesses almost crucifies him) and then the three of us sit there like the three wise monkeys. Finally, to force the situation, I go to the loo and think about Sylvia Plath and Ted Hughes until I, quite cold-bloodedly, get the tears to fall. I storm back to our table and announce that I'm leaving and of course he perks up like nobody's business. He bodily prevents me from leaving and Johnny (who didn't know where to put himself by now) insists that we sort things out. I can't remember who decided (though I fear, inevitably, that it was me) to split up and just be friends.

On the way to the West End the gloves come off. He suddenly admits that he was using me. All my doubts about feeling worthless had suddenly come true. I knew that if he hadn't been on the rebound then none of it would have happened. He wanted me to say things that would indicate that he'd really hurt me, but by this stage I wasn't particularly hurt, rather congratulating myself that I'd had a lucky escape.

Up West all the pubs were full. Johnny and I kept pretending that we were going to go to a gay club and in the end we decided to go back to the pub. He stormed off ahead and wouldn't sit next to us on the tube, so Johnny and I decided that we should go to our respective homes and he got off the train at Camden. I was left with a furious ex-boyfriend who accused me of ignoring him all evening and of trying to lure him into a gay club, and we ended up having a full-scale row, much to the delight of our fellow passengers. He insisted that we should both pretend to be happy even if we didn't feel happy which I said was banal and pointless. As we got off the tube I announced that I was going home. I think he was more annoyed that his New Year's Eve was ruined than anything else. Every time I went in the direction of a mini-cab office, he'd call me back to try and persuade me to go to the pub with him. I became terribly humble and tired with it all and started muttering apologies; 'I'm sorry I ruined your New Year's Eve. I'm sorry about everything, like it's all my fault.' Then he said, 'When you've finished with my videos let me know.' I ran into the cab office; he called me but I was too angry.

As I was driven home I could see him walking to the pub. I went home with 40 minutes to go until count-down, to fall on my bed with sobs and vow that I would never, ever, ever let anyone near.

Three weeks later he phoned and asked me out for a drink which I declined. I started to tell him that we'd both been lucky and that we'd have got all f∗∗∗ed up and hurt if we'd kept it going any longer and we could still be friends. (Stop me if you think that you've heard this one before.) He said that that kind of arrangement had never worked in the past and that since New Year's Eve he'd been a total recluse and that if I thought it was lucky, that was just my opinion. Does it sound like he still fancies me? I've written to him extending the hand of friendship and trying to arrange a time to return his oh so precious video-tapes, but he hasn't replied.

Despite this, things have started looking up from today. I've got an interview at the University of Sussex for their English and Media Studies degree. At the moment I'm working as a Brochure Despatch Clerk for a firm that specialises in walking holidays for geriatrics. My colleague is a big-headed, mercenary, lazy Olympic swimmer who does half the work I do for a third more money. He's just been given a major bollocking for bossing me about, so ha!

I know I've unburdened myself to you and even if you think it's just prattle it has helped to get it *all* down and I found that I could laugh at some bits. You're a boy, so tell me how you think he feels about me and comment where you see fit. Also enclosed for your delectation is the long-awaited compilation tape. I expect correspondence before 18 February. I think the only way to get letters from you at reasonable interludes is to set you deadlines!

Love,
SARRA xxxx

*Having just finished her GCSEs when she met her boyfriend Will, Bidisha had to fit him in with two more sets of exams, a career in journalism and writing a novel – not surprisingly, he didn't always come top priority . . .*

## Bidisha, aged 15–17

Thursday 21 July, 1994

Incredible. The weirdest day. It started off really badly, hearing I hadn't got the writing jobs I wanted from *NME* – they said they'd sent other people to review Oasis, and that I'd missed the rush to get on to the press party visiting Bjork's gig in Blackpool. Sat on the exercise bike and pedalled for forty minutes because I was so angry. Then Suzy called to invite me to a party held by *The Idler* magazine. Wore a short white silky dress and seemed to get on with people. Met someone – Will – and I'd never thought a man could be beautiful until I saw him. I was practically dribbling. We all went somewhere else after the party – to a drinking club, then Bar Italia. Suddenly, me and him found ourselves staring at each other for, Suzy says, about a minute, totally transfixed. It was certainly 'something' at first sight.

Saturday 30 July

Wake up at Suzy's place in Hampstead after my birthday meal. I'm 16 now – it doesn't feel any different. Still can't get served legally, etc. I know this thing with Will is going to be something interesting. Arrive home to find a postcard from him, wishing me a happy birthday. I try to call him, he isn't in. Perhaps I'm just being stupid.

## Tuesday 2 August

Woke up, met up with Suzy and her friend Katie. I wore the white dress that I met Will in (it is now one of my lucky garments) and had a bottle of wine and three double bourbons. I confess – I puked up. Everywhere. Several times. Oh well, good for tolerance. We went to the ICA – everything was already out of focus – and Suzy spent the evening talking to some shaven-headed jerk called Rob. He spent the whole time with glazed eyes, looking over her shoulder.

## Wednesday 3 August

Woke up at Suzy's wanting to die. Had cappuccino, still wanted to die. We went into the McDonald's in Hampstead, Suzy offered me a Bacon McMuffin and I almost puked again.

## Wednesday 10 August

Everything's total shit. No love life to speak of, no writing work. NME are still messing about – I worked out how much they owed me in unprinted work and faxed them about it. The response was cold to say the least. I thought this summer would be spent going out to parties and gigs, meeting people and working while waiting for my GCSE results. But it hasn't turned out that way. All I do is hang around with Suzy, eat, spend money I haven't got and whinge to Mum. I'm so bored. School begins in a few weeks' time and I'm actually looking forward to it. This summer's been a total waste of time. I'm so out of shape.

## Tuesday 27 December

Shopped, went to see Will for an hour, then had dinner

with Jodie. Covent Garden is strange and empty, just a few people out shopping in the sales. Will and I – don't know what's happening. It's obvious something's there but I feel too young around him. I can't think of anything to say, and when I speak it comes out in this stupid strangled kind of voice. My sense of humour must have evaporated or something. Wish I could skip ten or so years and then re-enter life in my mid-twenties. Dinner with Jodie was great, though. We went to a vegetarian Indian place, and (apparently) I got drunk and started going on about how totally beautiful Will is. Oops.

Saturday 14 January, 1995
End of first week back at school – I've put on weight and I'm totally unfit. Every morning Angela and I go down to the vending machine and have a choc bar and a pack of crisps each, washed down with extra-black coffee. So far I've become fixated upon Dimes, Drifters and Toffos, although right now it's a Lion Bar for me. Also, can't stop thinking about Will. It's odd. I don't know him, I don't even like him that much, but it feels as though my brain's full of him. I hope this isn't what relationships are like – full of unrealised, unfocused longing. Haven't done anything about it though. I'm sure the feeling isn't mutual.

Later: Oops, couldn't help it. Me and Jodie met at lunchtime today and I wrote him a note. I just saw some of his writing published today, so I said I was dropping a line of congrats and re-acquaintanceship. It's strange, it feels as though I'm being compelled to get in touch, as though there's no other option.

## Thursday 23 March

Haven't written for a while. Things have hit the wrong note. I'm finding things out about myself that I didn't know before. Will and I see each other once a week, though at the moment he's away on business. As soon as I started seeing him properly I realised a few things: firstly, that I don't think I'm cut out for relationships. I can't connect with people. I can't get close to them. Instead, it seems we're just acting out roles. I can't be myself around him, and he obviously thinks I'm a brainless girl. And he's so dumb! All he can talk about is parties, clubs, clothes — he's nearly 40 for God's sake. He thinks he's a hot-shot because he's bopped his life away. No wonder he doesn't have any brain cells left. But the thing is, I still like his looks, and I still have that instinct: that this is happening for a reason.

## Sunday 26 March

Can't stand this. Can't connect with people. Have to get out of this. He's thick, thick, thick. I have jokes with Angela about how stupid it is: that I could memorise the contents of the Qu'ran, and rewrite it, backwards, with each letter a different colour, using a quill pen, in the time it takes for him to string together an interesting sentence.

## Thursday 30 March

Sent him a fax saying I was too bored to see him any more. I've sent back some stuff he gave me — a Valentine's card a tape, some other things.

Sunday 7 May
I'm totally burnt thanks to sitting out on Primrose Hill with Suzy, eating ice cream. Still haven't done any work for school yet. I haven't seen Will for six weeks. He'd got the fax and called. We met up and he had a stupid tantrum in the middle of Patisserie Valerie. His pride was hurt. He told me, 'You can't talk to me the way you talk to your parents.' What an idiot. Okay, I admit I called a few days ago. Luckily we've got that number-withholding thing so he couldn't tell when I hung up on his voice. Phew. Don't know what made me call, though.

Tuesday 9 May
He called at ten-thirty tonight. Actually, he called and hung up on my voice, but I called him back. Evidently he hasn't mastered the number-withholding thing. Sadly things didn't go too well. I hung up.

Wednesday 10 May
People talk about heartache cynically. But your heart really does hurt. Spent the day at school grouching and eating choc. Called him tonight. After two seconds he hangs up on me. This is becoming a battle of egos, and I still don't feel we're any closer to knowing each other. I just can't engage with people: I'm frightened of it.

Saturday 16 September
Haven't written for a while – I've started working like mad for the Oxford entrance exams, which are in November. I'm reading a book and a half a day. I've given up choc and coffee in favour of a few pages of morning reading in the library. I'm not stressed, though, just

working hard. I haven't seen Will since his tantrum in the spring, although we have kept in touch through phone calls. We've got closer and closer but we're still too nervous to see each other. It keeps reminding me of Beatrice and Benedick in *Much Ado About Nothing*. What if it doesn't work out?

What must it be like to be nearly 40 and still single? He's wasted his life. Well anyway, last night, after a year and a half of this, I called him. We spoke for hours and it is the breaking-point. We admitted our feelings and wondered what to do. I decided to end it. I've got this incredible book deal – should be hearing from my editor any day now, after spending one of my best summers writing my novel – and I also have journalism, Oxbridge, school. Love is the lowest priority at the moment.

Sunday 17 September
So, it's Sunday. Feel crap. No sooner do we admit something's there than it ceases to exist.

Sunday 1 October
Am only thinking about work, now. Only five weeks until the exams and I can't stop reading and eating, usually at the same time. Everyone I know who's doing Oxbridge is the same.

Thursday 5 October
Have taken a day off to recover from an evening with Suzy, a bottle of red wine and a few dishes of Korean food. If I stop now, though, my energy levels will hit a real low. I must work!

Tuesday 24 October

I'm beginning to panic a bit now. If I don't finish Dickens and Hardy by tomorrow, I'll be seriously behind. Only now am I beginning to put the last year and a half into perspective and I feel Will and I just took the easy option and let things go. It's better to regret doing something than regret not having done something: it's a cliché, yeah, but . . . well. Too late. I didn't even like him. Must read *The Mayor of Casterbridge*.

Friday 15 December

I can't believe it. I got into Oxford! Passed the exam, then went through three hellish interviews. I got the letter this morning, and only now realise how badly I wanted to get in. My good friends Maya and Danielle, and several others, have also got in. This is what I wanted. This makes the split with Will worth it. I've got an unconditional offer so I don't need to worry about 'A' levels, technically, although mocks are in January and I'd still like to get good grades in the summer.

Thursday 13 April, 1996

Things are going very, very badly. I haven't revised at quite the pace I should have. I have to either learn Spanish or get my notes in order and memorise like a parrot. My agent has, I assume, returned from a trip to New York but hasn't been in touch. I haven't heard from the publishers either. Very, very bad. I spend all my time worrying about office politics and my career: this isn't how my life was supposed to be. All I've done in a year and a half is work. The editor at my publishers has left, and my book might fall through the gap as they try and reorganise things. I can't get journalistic work. I gave up the chance of something good, just for this unhappiness? Exams are a week away and I can't do anything. I'm just sitting here looking at the books and daydreaming. Am putting on weight, and have big tits, big arse and no waist – like a pregnant Shetland pony.

Thursday 6 June
Cannot believe what I have just done. Sat down to my first history exam totally prepared, looked at the word 'Stalin' and, somehow, thought it said 'Mussolini'. Wrote entire essay about Italian foreign policy. I must be going bonkers. Optical illusion hell. I failed, failed, failed. Not that it matters, I only have to get two E's for uni, but – argh!

Saturday 8 June
Am shell-shocked. Last night, in the middle of a crashing storm, he called. I was in bed trying to see the funny side of the Mussolini débâcle, and worrying about editing my novel. I hadn't spoken to him in six months. He told me he was going to leave London for good, and set up home in Paris. He's so obviously sad, it's as though he's tried every route to happiness here, and it hasn't worked. So he's going to try and be happy in another country. Part of me desperately wanted to tell him to stay, but the greater part thinks that too much time has passed. I was held back by my ambivalence, and managed to say in that strangled nutcase voice: 'Well, all the best!'

Oxford starts in October, the novel is on its way, I'm meeting Jodie for dinner tonight. It's time to close the door on the past.

*Kate Cann's diary extracts show her discovering what she wants from a relationship, and then trying to get it. From her relationship with Harry – who adores her, but whom she doesn't really fancy – to the beginning of a relationship with Mark – who isn't a safe option, but is gorgeous – she charts the ups and downs of a complex love life! This situation was later to inspire her novels* Diving In *and* In the Deep End, *as Coll chooses between sensible Greg and sexy Art . . .*

## Kate Cann, aged 17

2 January, 1972

Harry has just phoned saying he hates feeling unsure of me and he isn't sure of me any more. What right has he got to have me safe, in a pocket? He wants to understand me then tape me up, so that I can't change any more but can just sit there and love him. Everything I say or do he construes in terms of himself. When I told him about the two occasions I was asked out by other people, but didn't go, he said – 'Thank you. That's a compliment to me.' But it was *not* a compliment to him – it was all *me*, my decision, because I didn't *want* to go out with them, because I didn't like them! In his mind he knows he is right, he absolutely believes he feels the right emotions at the right times, although he does like talking about his failings too, finishing with a complacent – 'Well, that's me, I suppose – I'd like to be like you but I can't.'

The truth is he would not like to be like me at *all*. He thinks we have such a wonderful relationship, but how can we have when my slightest remark is enough to send him scurrying to hide behind his principles and what I may have once said, because ideas, of course, may not be changed . . . I hate the way things are turning out at the moment, me in the role of never-satisfied, bitching, criticising female, and him as the poor lad forced to change his character. He makes such a *point* of it.

I can't stand it when everything I say, think, do, want or need he takes as reflecting on him and utterly involving him. It doesn't. I must be separate and free to give him what I want to give him because I want to give it to him, not because I'm required to by convention as a girlfriend. Some of the things he's said have really jerked me. When he said he didn't want to 'share me' with anyone else, as though I was food; when he said he was only jealous of boys where I was concerned, but he could be of girls too – 'If you were having some deep discussion with some girl on Christianity or something I'd get angry because I'd think you should be talking to me.'

28 January
Do I love Harry? He has said he loves me, in all seriousness, and I believe he really does or at least really thinks he does. I'm not sure, but then I never am of anything important. I know how destroyed and upset I would be if he left me – as though a huge part of me had gone – but wouldn't there also be a feeling of relief that I was on my own and all my own again, independent, aloof, touching no one?

4 February
His ideals and notions are so limited. Just when I'm beginning to get roused and passionate he's yawning and ready to chuck me out of the car because he'd said he wouldn't be late home. He won't entertain any idea of

defying Mummy and Daddy for me — yes, he wants to go on holiday with me because that's what John did with Sandra and anyway, everyone thinks he sleeps with me, but Mum and Dad mustn't know ... He's getting boring, I swear he is. If only he knew what I was thinking as I sit there and listen to him.

11 February

I don't want to lose this feeling. I feel that at long last, I'm in love with Harry! I really can't stop thinking about him; last night we went to Steve and Michelle's engagement party and had a great time, and I just wanted to be with him, and we kept separating and coming together naturally. There was no idea of his 'hanging round me' any more — he went with his friends, I with mine, and I just was not ashamed to be with him; I liked it, despite the fact that superior-ex Andy was there ...

I'm so changeable. I can't decide whether this new feeling I have for Harry — that he is all I want — is really new, or rather old but I never recognised it — or whether it's just me changing about again, soon to dislike him. All I know is, he no longer seems inferior in any way to me. I am proud we are such an equal couple; I no longer have that hideous feeling of praying he won't make a fool of me ...

Oh, I love Harry — now I've stopped stamping on him and he is sure of me, we get on so beautifully! I wish I could stop having moods. When we were in Southend, sitting on the seafront, and he was naming the stars, it was so gorgeous.

4 March

We had another chance to sleep together yesterday. We

went round to his house – everyone was out. We got on the bed, he undid my T-shirt and he took his shirt off, but I didn't want to – neither of us were turned on. He said 'I still wish you were on the pill' and whoosh, I just wanted to get dressed and get out. I don't care about loving, friendly, liberated friendships any more. I felt humiliated and enraged . . . I want more passion, less reverence . . .

I hate it when he says 'I understand you, you're so straightforward and logical' – I'm *anything* but, I *know* I'm not. He thinks I am because I come over strong; he thinks he's complex because he's muddled and muddied. He likes to think he's got me taped; he doesn't want to understand me. I'd like to get that loving, giving letter I wrote him and tear it up under his nose.

I'm so furious and confused I can't set down anything clearly. I don't even believe I want to be clear. I am in an emotionally dead limbo.

## 10 March

Four days now since we split up. What amazes me is how everything reminds me of him, ceaselessly. Like a sharp kick – I'll never see him again. Just now I put on an old jacket of his and the effect that the male smell had on me was quite amazing and animal – if anyone thinks their head rules their senses they should be in a situation like this! Songs remind me because I remember what he has said about them. My handbag is full of tickets and things – a programme from 'Behind the Fridge' – things we went to see together. When Jane suggested we go to Petticoat Lane I felt a tug – because I'd intended to buy him one of those weird and cheap little glass ornaments when I went there again. Every article of clothing I have reminds me heavily of Harry — I can remember the occasions I wore them and what he said about them. . . he loved all my rings. He used to borrow my two jokey Rupert badges and wear them to school.

. . . It was horrible, like a nightmare, on Wednesday. For as long as I can remember, practically, he has wanted to go out with me and get seriously involved. It was me who always held back and went out on my own. Now suddenly he said — he realised he didn't want to get involved at all. It was all too much for him. He said another six months and he'd want to marry me, and he'd never known anyone else; he had to be free to go out with other girls. He was seriously involved with me and this had jeopardised his work and his future, which he said was all important to him. He thought of me all the time and this stopped his work. He said he wished he could just wipe the last year out, he was in too deep, he needed drastic action to yank him out, and this was us breaking up. I was desperate and hopeful by turns. I can remember feeling angry that it was him saying this to me, when it was always usually the other way round, and I'd assumed I'd leave him. I kicked the car and yelled SHIT! — I burst into tears and shook him off when he tried to comfort me. I wouldn't take his handkerchief. I remember feeling a kind of huge and desperate relief; I also remember having to stop myself from pleading with him not to leave me.

. . . I was furious that he, the more besotted of us two, could find the strength to be so final and decisive when all I could do was waffle and moan, feel disgruntled, pick fights, get dreary and muddle along until I was finally thrown out.

**16 March**

I have been waiting all day to get home and write in this book. I've spent today with all my feelings about Harry roused up again. Sally told me that Pam had heard Harry was going out with Juliet. He must have asked her the day after I said I didn't want us to 'still be friends', but to have a complete split, on the phone. I felt vaguely sick, I got back the feeling in my stomach, I felt furious with him . . . How ordinary he was being, how cheap, treating his love for me as some kind of digestion complaint that must be cured by lots of exercise, cold baths, Juliet and nights out with the lads . . . How can he be so weak – so much for his valued freedom – going out with a girl he doesn't even like? . . . I *know* that he feels nothing for her and never could . . . He'll go back to being safe and chatty and narrow without me. I want him to suffer; I want him to sit there in the car with her and think how different I was, and how dead she is, how unexciting and self-conscious with that long, superior nose and grey eyeshadow. I want him to see me out with a good-looking bloke, I want him to see me enjoying myself and I want him to suffer with regret that he's smashed it all because he was a coward about the future.

**17 March**

Stuart is having a party this Saturday, and I've been asked, and it's likely that Mark will be there, who is apparently very tall and beautiful, like a stretched out and rejuvenated Marc Bolan. This is exactly what I need both to take my mind off Harry and to test my feelings on Harry . . .

18 March – 3.15 am

. . . The whole evening was spent in our discussing how sordid everyone else was, lunging at each other, how we just wanted casual friends and to go out with lots of people, how bored we were with boy-girlfriend relationships. Mark seems to have lines of girlfriends all doting on him and all getting laid by him. He seems to want a girl he can really like, he despises girls in general. The thing is, I feel bored with the prospect of it all somehow . . .

19 March

Even if I never see Mark again, the prospect of which doesn't please me but doesn't leave me desolate either, I shall be grateful for having met him. He's shown me that Harry was not someone exceptional in that we too could talk so easily and that he had ideas like mine . . . that I can spend an evening with someone whom I find interesting, lively, warm and more attractive than Harry (aaagh – I've said it – SIN! But it's true. Mark has the face of a demonic cherub and such lovely *bones*) . . .

20 March

I feel as though I am bursting with a huge, all-embracing energy. I want to do thousands of things, make things happen . . . I feel free, independent and so sure of myself . . . I feel I must strip myself down to the nerve ends so I can be absolutely aware. I want to be involved with everything, I want to stir people and listen and learn, absorb and give out too. I feel I could wrench people's heads open and investigate their brains and rearrange them and put them back (with their approval, of course).

20 March — but later on . . .

A few hours ago I wanted to shout scream kick the house down for sheer triumph and joy. I felt so full I was exploding, delirious, gorgeous. Even now I can't prevent a huge, smug, blissful smile from taking over my face completely!

I got a phone call from Mark . . .

# Biographical Notes

*Joan Aiken* was born in Rye, Sussex, in 1924. She is the daughter of American poet Conrad Aiken and Canadian Jessie McDonald. She was educated at home until the age of 12 and then boarded at Wychwood School, Oxford. She left school in 1941 to work at the BBC. She has also worked as a librarian in charge of documents at the United Nations London Information Centre, as a features editor at *Argosy* magazine and at an advertising agency. In 1961 she started writing full time and has now written over 100 books. She lives in Sussex with her husband.

*Judy Allen* was born in 1941 in Old Sarum, Wiltshire, and was an only child. After her father's death she and her mother moved in with her grandparents and lived with them on and off for some years. She worked in various jobs – in shops, in the offices of theatres, in a literary agency, as an editor in a publishing house and as a freelance editor and writer – before becoming a full-time writer in the 1980s. She has published over 50 books, fiction and non-fiction, and has had four radio plays and two radio dramatisations broadcast. Her novel *Awaiting Developments* won the Whitbread Children's Award in 1988 and the Friends of the Earth Earthworm Award in 1989, and *Tiger* won The Washington Children's Choice Award in 1995.

*Bidisha Bandyopadhyay* was born in London in 1978. She has worked as a journalist for *Dazed and Confused*, *i-D*, *The Big Issue* and *NME*. Her first novel, *Seahorses,* was published in May 1997 and was featured as Début of the Month in Dillons. Her second novel, *The One*, is forthcoming. She is currently in her second year on scholarship at Oxford University.

*Charlotte Brontë* was born in 1816, the fourth of six children, including Emily and Anne Brontë. She attended boarding school at Cowan Bridge and later at Roe Head, which she returned to as a teacher. She also worked as a private governess before going to Brussels with Emily in 1842 to study languages. In 1846, Charlotte published a book containing her own, Emily and Anne's poetry, using male pseudonyms – the book only sold two copies! In this year she also wrote her first novel, *The Professor*, which wasn't published until after her death. However, her second novel *Jane Eyre* was published the next year, in 1847, and was a great success. She went on to write and publish *Shirley* (1849) and *Villette* (1853) and was known as an extraordinarily talented writer, though some critics accused her of being too 'strong minded' and 'coarse' for a woman. She turned down all offers of marriage until 1854 when she married AB Nicholls, her father's curate. Charlotte Brontë died in childbirth in 1855.

*Kate Cann* lives in Twickenham with her husband, daughter, son and dog. She worked as a book editor for many years before writing *Diving In* (Livewire, 1996) and *In the Deep End* (Livewire, 1997). She has also written two novels for the young adult list at Red Fox, and a book in the Life Education series for Watts publishers.

*Charlotte Cooper* is a writer whose work has appeared in anthologies, magazines, zines and academic journals. She is the author of *Fat and Proud: The Politics of Size* (The Women's Press, 1998). She lives in the East End of London.

*Yvonne Coppard* was born in 1955 and grew up in Middlesex. She was a teacher for many years, and then became an advisory teacher in Child Protection for the Education Authority in Cambridge, where she now lives. Yvonne is married to Reg and they have two daughters – Naomi and Sophie. She is the author of ten books including *Bully* and *Not Dressed Like That, You Don't*.

*Eileen Fairweather* was brought up in North London. Her father was a policeman, her mother a school dinner lady, and she was educated at a girls' convent grammar school. She read English at the University of Sussex.

She acted in fringe theatre for two years, helped edit a feminist publication, and has written for numerous newspapers and magazines and worked on TV documentaries. She specialises in social affairs. She won the Catherine Pakenham Award for young women journalists in 1983, and in 1993 and 1996 won British Press Awards for Investigative Journalism, with London *Evening Standard* colleague Stewart Payne, for exposing the abuse of children in care. Her Livewire novels, *French Letters: The Lives and Loves of Miss Maxine Harrison* (1987) and *French Leave: Maxine Harrison Moves Out!* (1996), have been translated into many languages.

*Anne Frank* was born in Frankfurt-am-Main, Germany in 1929. She fled from the Nazis to Holland in 1933 with her family. During the Nazi occupation of Holland she hid with her family and four others in the sealed-off back room of an office in Amsterdam – from 1942 until they were betrayed in August 1944. She died in Belsen concentration camp.

*Juliet Gellatley* went vegetarian at 15 years old and has spent most of her life fighting for animals. After her degree in zoology and psychology she became the Vegetarian Society's first Youth Education Officer and rose to be its Director. On the way, she launched Britain's first-ever youth campaign against factory farming, increasing the number of schools offering veggie meals from 13 per cent to 65 per cent, and launched *Greenscene*, Britain's only magazine for young vegetarians. In October 1994 she launched *Viva!*, an exciting new vegetarian and vegan charity for adults and young people.

She is the author of *The Livewire Guide to Going, Being, and Staying Veggie!* (Livewire, 1996).

*Sarra Manning* was born and lives in London. She is currently Senior Writer at *J17* and has previously written for *Melody Maker*. She is also a regular contributor to *Select, Minx* and *SKY*. Her first book, *Love Money,* was published in February 1998. She is currently working on a second novel, *The Star Tripper*.

*Katherine Mansfield* was born in Wellington, New Zealand in 1888 to a middle-class colonial family, the third of six children. As a teenager she attended Queen's College in London before returning to New Zealand in 1906. She persuaded her family to let her go back to London in 1908. Her friends included Virginia Woolf and DH Lawrence and she married magazine editor John Middleton Murray. Her first book of short stories was published in 1909 and she went on to write several collections of short stories, poems and a novella, all of which contributed significantly to the literary movement modernism. From 1910 she suffered from ill health and she spent much of her later years writing while convalescing in France. She died in 1923.

*Millie Murray* was born in London, in 1958, of Jamaican parentage. A qualified nurse, she has attended drama college, worked with several black theatre workshops, and been a vocalist in a gospel choir. She created the radio sit-com, *The Airport*; has written for the television series, *The Real McCoy*; and facilitates writing and performance workshops throughout the country.

She is the author of the popular Livewire novels *Kiesha* (1988), *Lady A – A Teenage DJ* (1989), *Cairo Hughes* (1996) and *Sorrelle* (1998) as well as *All About Jas, Ebony and the Mookatoor Bush* and *Addicted* (with Steve Derbyshire).

*Sylvia Plath* was born in 1932 in Boston, USA. She had early writing success, with poems and short stories published while at Smith College, as well as winning the *Ms* magazine College Fiction Contest. The pressure of maintaining her high level of achievements led to a breakdown while at college, and her experiences of this time are fictionalised in the novel *The Bell Jar* (1963). After her recovery she gained an honours degree and then went on to study at Cambridge University, England. Here she met and married the poet Ted Hughes with whom she had two children. As well as her novel she wrote many poems – collected in the volumes *The Colossus and Other Poems* (1962) and *Ariel* (1965) – and short stories. Sylvia Plath committed suicide in 1963 at the age of 30.

*Christine Purkis* lives in Bristol where she taught for 15 years before a serious illness prompted her to concentrate on her earlier love of writing. Her first novel, *Peta's Pence*, was published by Livewire in 1990. Four more novels have since been published by The Bodley Head – *The Shuttered Room*, *Sea Change*, *Dark Beneath the Moon* and *Paddlefeet*.

*May Sarton* was born in Belgium in 1912, and emigrated to America with her parents in 1914 as refugees from World War I. She was the daughter of English artist and designer Eleanor Mabel Elwes Sarton and historian of science and Harvard professor, George Sarton. May began writing poetry at 9. She worked as an Apprentice in Eva LeGallienne's Civic Associated Actors Theatre in New York for four years before founding her own

Associated Actors Theatre, which failed during the depression; at that time May became a full time writer with the publication of her first volume of poetry in 1937 at the age of 25. It was then that she came to England and formed lifelong friendships with Elizabeth Bowen, Juliette and Julian Huxley, Virginia Woolf, Vita Sackville-West and many others. Although she never attended college, May went on to teach at Harvard University and Radcliffe College, as well as colleges and universities throughout the United States. An acclaimed poet, novelist and keeper of journals, by the time of her death at 83 in 1995, May had published 55 volumes including the novel *Kinds of Love* (The Women's Press, 1995) and her bestselling *Journal of a Solitude* (The Women's Press, 1985), and earned 18 honorary degrees as well as countless humanitarian awards. *May Sarton: Selected Letters 1916–1954*, edited by Susan Sherman, was published by The Women's Press in 1997.

*Mary Wollstonecraft Shelley*, born in 1797, was the daughter of feminist Mary Wollstonecraft and rationalist philosopher William Godwin. Her mother died a few days after her birth, leaving Mary to educate herself amongst her father's intellectual circle. In 1812, she met Percy Bysshe Shelley and in 1814 they eloped, travelling through France, Switzerland and Germany and jointly recording their experience in *History of a Six Weeks Tour* (1817). They returned to England and Mary gave birth to a son. They spent the summer of 1816 with Lord Byron and Claire Clairmont on Lake Geneva, and this is where she began her novel *Frankenstein* (1818). They returned to England and married on the death of Shelley's first wife, and went to live in Italy in 1818. The next few years were fraught – two of Mary's children died as well as Shelley, and she suffered a miscarriage. However, she returned to England in 1822 determined not to remarry, but to make her own living and support her remaining child by writing novels. This she did until her death in 1851.

*Tamara Sturtz* was born in Leamington Spa in 1968 and moved to Bath in 1983. She studied Fashion Journalism at the London Institute and has worked on various magazines, including *Marie Claire* and *Harpers & Queen*, and is currently Beauty Editor at *Minx*. Tamara lives in Notting Hill, London, but plans to move to Halki, a very tiny Greek island, to write novels and marry a Greek fisherman!

*Virginia Woolf* was born in London in 1882. She was educated at home and in 1904, at the age of 22, she began a career in literary journalism. Her first novel, *The Voyage Out*, appeared in 1915, and her subsequent works include *Mrs Dalloway* (1925) and *To the Lighthouse* (1927). Virginia Woolf also wrote two major non-fiction works, *A Room of One's Own* (1929) and *Three Guineas* (1938). Throughout her life Virginia Woolf maintained a reputation as a literary critic, and reviewed an astonishing number of works for *The Times Literary Supplement* and other journals. In addition to her literary and critical work she invested considerable time in writing letters and a diary. She was highly critical of the society in which she lived, refusing to accept honours from either the state or universities. In 1912 she married Leonard Woolf and in 1917 they founded The Hogarth Press, which published the early work of writers such as TS Eliot, Katherine Mansfield and Sigmund Freud. The Woolfs lived in London for much of their lives, in the area between King's Cross and the British Museum which is designated 'Bloomsbury', and at Rodmell in Sussex.

# grab a livewire!
### real life, real issues, real books, real bite

Rebellion, rows, love and sex . . . pushy boyfriends, fussy parents, infuriating brothers and pests of sisters . . . body image, trust, fear and hope . . . homelessness, bereavement, friends and foes . . . raves and parties, teachers and bullies . . . identity, culture clash, tension and fun . . . abuse, alcoholism, cults and survival . . . fat thighs, hairy legs, hassle and angst . . . music, black issues, media and politics . . . animal rights, environment, veggies and travel . . . taking risks, standing up, shouting loud and breaking out . . .

### . . . grab a Livewire!

For a free copy of our latest catalogue,
send a stamped addressed envelope to:

**The Sales Department**
**Livewire Books**
**The Women's Press Ltd**
**34 Great Sutton Street**
**London EC1V 0DX**
**Tel: 0171 251 3007**
**Fax: 0171 608 1938**

## Also of interest:

Sandra Chick

## Cheap Street

'When we part, it's with few words that don't mean anything. See you soon, take care, and all that rubbish. I walk home the long way. Avoiding the places I've seen Kelly's sister hanging out, on account I don't want my face smashed in. Stand on the bridge. Looking back towards home. Wondering — when I'll see me mum again. Feeling beaten up and angry inside.'

Somewhere between the labour ward and the benefit office, Lisa Brunt's mother lost her spark. Lisa's determined that won't happen to her. But how do you carve out a life for yourself if you're stuck on a run-down housing estate, your clothes are scruffy, you're not skinny enough, and your mum's gone off with Dan the Man? Lisa takes it day by day, surrounded by cheap food, cheap clothes, cheap fags, cheap living, as she looks for a way off Cheap Street . . .

'Utterly believable and very compelling.' *The Times*

'Coherent and powerful.' *Times Literary Supplement*

Fiction £4.99
ISBN 0 7043 4949 3

Millie Murray
**Sorrelle**

Sorrelle has always told everyone that she would only go out with a black boy. There are enough people saying black isn't beautiful and if you went out with someone who wasn't black that was just showing you agreed with them. But then Sorrelle meets Arun, the gorgeous Asian boy that everyone seems to fancy.

Before she knows it, Sorrelle has agreed to go out with Arun and finds that she likes him very much. But everyone seems to be against them. Soon Sorrelle is dealing with warring parents and a furious best friend, and hostility from just about everyone else. As she tries to sort out her own mixed feelings and swirling emotions, Sorrelle finds herself asking why there is such a gulf between black and Asian people and whether bridges between them can ever be built . . .

**'Over the past few years, Millie Murray has been quietly building a reputation as one of the foremost writers of teenage fiction.'** *Caribbean Times*

Fiction  £4.99
ISBN  0 7043 4954 X

Eileen Fairweather

**French Letters**
**The Life and Loves of Miss Maxine Harrison**

'Dear Jean,

Since you deserted London to live in the middle of
nowhere I've cried non-stop. Mum says I'll soon find
another best friend, but that just goes to show she's got
no heart.

Yes, I did ask mum if she'd adopt you, but she says the
law wouldn't allow it seeing as you're already fourteen
and you belong to someone else. Trust her to take the
easy way out.'

Maxine's got Real Problems. She's broke, forever on a diet, and
now her best friend's moved miles away. But at least they can
write . . .

Through hilarious letters, Maxine and Jean share their
struggles with unfair parents, snobbish schoolmates, a rotten
sister and a creep of a brother. And make a mega-mess of
relationships with boys . . .

'Hugely enjoyable.' *British Book News*

'Compulsively witty.' *Times Literary Supplement*

'Very funny.' *Observer*

Fiction £4.99
ISBN 0 7043 4951 5

# grab a livewire!
## save £££s!!! with this voucher

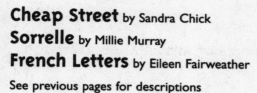

Buy any of the following books and get
**£1 off each book you buy! Post-free!**

**Cheap Street** by Sandra Chick
**Sorrelle** by Millie Murray
**French Letters** by Eileen Fairweather

See previous pages for descriptions

**Name** ——————————————————————————
**Address** ————————————————————————
————————————————————————————————
————————————————————————————————
**Postcode** ————————————————————

I would like:

—— copies of **Cheap Street** at £4.99 less £1 = £3.99

—— copies of **Sorrelle** at £4.99 less £1 = £3.99

—— copies of **French Letters** at £4.99 less £1 = £3.99

—— Livewire catalogue

**Total enclosed £** _____

Do not send cash through the post. Send postal orders (from the Post Office)
in pounds sterling or cheques made out to The Women's Press.

Send this form and your cheque or postal order to The Women's Press,
34 Great Sutton Street, London EC1V 0DX. Allow up to 28 days for delivery.
**Do remember to fill in your name and address!**

This offer applies only in the UK to the books listed above, subject to availability.
This voucher cannot be exchanged for cash. Cash value 0.0001p